THE HISTORY LESSON

BRUCE F. KATZ

ISBN: 979-8-9875634-0-3 (paperback)
ISBN: 979-8-9875634-1-0 (ebook)

Also from Bruce F. Katz

Fiction

The Family Jewels

Non-Fiction

When Your Name is On the Door

PROLOGUE

Raymond wasn't sure if the tears making their way slowly down his cheeks were the result of joy at holding his four-month-old granddaughter or from sadness at the loss of his daughter, the baby's mother, from complications during the birth of this beautiful baby.

"Jonquil," he whispered. He repeated her name while he fed her, while he changed her, while she slept, even while she cried. Her mother had named her Jonquil, after the flower, just moments before she passed. Sometimes he called her Jonny, a nickname her father picked out for her. Raymond missed his own daughter every day; parents aren't supposed to outlive their children. He also felt blessed every day to be in his granddaughter's presence.

Raymond paced the room while holding his granddaughter, rocking her in his arms, talking to her, kissing her, like he did most every waking minute of each day. He took her everywhere with him. He took her to the supermarket on the edge of downtown Vosalia whenever he went to buy groceries. He took her when he walked the quarter mile up the driveway to pick up their mail, every day except Sunday. On Sundays, he took her to the AME church up the pike. All the women, young and old, oohed and aahed. They hugged him and smooched her. She was always quiet in church, as if she knew instinctively how to behave in God's house. She was the only female he knew who never showed him any sass. He suspected that would change with the passage of time.

Sometimes, when the weather didn't cooperate, he'd sit on the sofa with her in his arms and just talk to her. Maybe he needed to talk so he wouldn't be alone with his thoughts, fears, and memories. Especially the memories. He'd tell her stories; some he made up, others he culled from his own life. He believed she needed to know everything he could tell her. He talked to her often about her parents.

"Jonquil," he'd say, "your daddy is a very smart, very handsome young man. When you older, you will be a beautiful, strong, intelligent young woman. Your mama, Tonya, was the most beautiful, most loving girl God ever placed in northwestern Mississippi. I miss her so much, but your daddy, he'll be home later this year, and he'll make sure you have everything your sweet little heart desires. That is, if I don't get it for you first.

"Lemme tell you something about your daddy,

Jonquil. He's a big boy. Star running back at Pitts County High School, broke the single season rushing record down at Southern Mississippi, graduated from college, which a lot of athletes don't do, and enlisted in the US Marines. He probably could have been an officer if he went into the army, but he wanted the training that came with being a marine. When he comes home, you need to tell him, *oooo-rah!* He'll like that. Come on, Jonny, say it for me now . . . *oooo-rah!* Okay. Maybe later."

Other times, Raymond bragged shamelessly to Jonquil about his late wife, Jacinta, and their pride and joy, their daughter, Tonya. Tonya. That wound was still wide open.

"I'm real sorry you won't get to know your mama, Jonquil, or your grandma," he told her. "Your grandma was the apple of my eye, that's for sure. She poured most all her love into raising your mama. I say most because she held back a little bit, just for me."

Mostly, he talked to her because his deep voice seemed to soothe the baby. She'd occasionally reward him with a smile, a yawn, a burp, or something else that warmed his heart.

"I knew your grandma—she was my wife—from work and from church," he said. "She worked where I did, over at the mill, and she sang in the choir at our church. She was so pretty. After your mama was born, she took care of things here at the house while I worked." He paused for a moment and blinked back some tears. "She'd have been over the moon if she could've met you, Jonny. Over the moon! But cervical cancer took her in 1987 at forty-nine.

"Now your mama, her name was Tonya. She up in heaven with her mama, but she is watching out for you and your daddy, and maybe she's even keepin' an eye on your old granddaddy."

Jonquil presented him with a healthy burp, followed by a radiant smile. This sent Raymond into a fit of laughter. Other times, he'd weep, unashamedly. It didn't matter. He loved it when she let him know she was satisfied with her bottle of formula.

"Your mama was the prettiest flower in the garden," he said. "Yes, she was. She came back here after college and taught third grade at the elementary school 'til she and Marcus, that's your daddy's name, Marcus Carter, were ready to start a family of their own. You are the family they started, Jonquil. The alpha and the omega." He bit his lips.

Raymond spent hours, every day, filling Jonquil's head with pretty pictures and flowery stories about her family. He also told her about his own twenty-year career in the army: about the places he went, the people he met. He even told her about his time in Vietnam.

He knew a lot of people in Pitts County and a lot of people knew him, but he had always been quiet and thoughtful and didn't make friends easily. He kept his distance from most people, even after he retired and came home in 1977. He went to work at the mill and met and married Jacinta. If someone had asked back then if he could imagine himself, a quarter-century later, as sole guardian of a tiny baby girl, he'd have told the fool to go and get some help. But Raymond Steadman never saw profit in complaining about things over which he had no control. He'd played the cards he was dealt as best he could, and he'd let the chips fall wherever they happened to fall.

When Jonquil was ten-and-a-half months old, Raymond learned Marcus had died in Afghanistan. Marcus was one of twelve marines killed in action, probably by bullets from the same guns the US had sent to Afghanistan in the 1980s, when the people we were supporting, the Mujahideen, were at war with an invading army from the Soviet Union.

"Your daddy was a good man, Jonny, and I'm sure I'll tell you about him again, when you a few minutes older than you are now."

A game Raymond played with his granddaughter involved responding to an imaginary question posed whenever she made any sort of sound. "What's that, baby?" he'd ask her. "You want to know what baseball is? Okay, I'll tell you all about baseball, and then he'd set off on a stream-of-consciousness monologue in praise of the Atlanta Braves and their pitching staff.

It was in an answer to one of those imagined questions that Raymond, for the first time, when she was thirteen-months old, told Jonquil about a day seared into his memory.

He told her it was a day he first met someone he cared about deeply for many years even though they'd only spent a couple of innocent hours together, mostly playing cribbage. He told her it was a day he made an unlikely, lifelong friend at a time when such friendships could not and did not exist. And, he told her, he was wearing his army uniform, in his own hometown, and that, for no good reason, he almost lost his life.

"Lemme tell you all about that day, Jonny," he said. "It was May 26, 1960, a Thursday. I was home on leave from the army, and I was in town, here in Vosalia, to return a book I'd borrowed from the black high school library . . ."

CHAPTER 1

Fourteen Years Later
Wednesday, October 18

Jonquil jumped from her seat and leaped through the open door of the slow-rolling school bus. "Young lady," the driver shouted, "how many times I got to tell you? You need to wait until the bus comes to a full stop!"

She turned and smiled at him. "Then don't open the door till you come to a full stop, Mr. Williamson." He smiled back, shook his head, and dismissed her with a single wave of his right hand.

"Go ahead," he said. "Show me that four-hundred-meter form." The remaining students gathered into the seats and hung out the windows on the right side of the bus to watch Jonny run.

She looked up the long, straight, gravel-covered driveway lined with mature groundsel standing nearly two feet high. She put her backpack on, looked at her wristwatch, and sprinted up the driveway, gaining speed with each stride of her muscular legs. She barely broke a sweat under the early fall, midafternoon sun, finishing her quarter-mile run at three seconds over a minute. She jumped the four steps onto the front porch of her grandfather's shotgun bungalow.

Raymond was on the porch, getting the best out of his old, beat-up rocking chair. He smiled when Jonquil landed with a loud thump. Her face sported a wide, gap-toothed smile. It warmed his heart.

"How'd it go today, Jonny?" His left hand held out a red Solo cup filled with ice cubes and lemonade.

"Okay, Poppop, for a Monday," she said. She took the cup and swallowed a long guzzle. "We have an assignment to write a paper on something historical about Pitts County." She kissed his cheek and sat down next to him. "I think I'll write about you. You are nothin' if not historical."

He chuckled. "Yeah, well, if I'm historical, you're hysterical." She laughed. "Well, I guess there's some history in this poor excuse for a place," he said, "but I can't figure out what all it might be that would make it worth a whole school paper."

"I gotta pee," she said, squeezing another smile out of him. "Think about it for a minute."

The screen door slammed behind her. She bounded up the stairs. "Girl makes more noise than a whole herd o' horses," he said aloud.

He loved her with his whole heart, and he loved

having her around. He couldn't imagine how lonely his existence might be without being able to watch her grow into the woman he knew she was destined to become.

"A whole herd?" she asked, returning to the porch with six Oreo cookies, four for her, and two for him.

Raymond took in Jonny's appearance. God, the girl was getting tall, just like her mama. Almost fifteen and nearly five feet ten in bare feet, actually two inches taller than her mother when Tonya was full grown. She showed no body fat at all. He couldn't imagine she'd grow much more, but her father topped out at six three, and everyone else in her bloodline was over average height, so who knew? Her facial features resembled those of her ancestors. She was a strikingly beautiful young woman. Her spirit was upbeat and joyful, despite the circumstances of her childhood.

Raymond knew he had done a darned good job bringing her up to this point. He accepted as gospel truth that Jonquil's mere existence was the sole reason he was able and willing to get out of bed every morning.

She was long, lean, and athletic to her core. She had stellar academics, a deadly three-point shot, and was friends with almost everyone, boys and girls, black and white. She smiled easily and made those around her smile as well. In Raymond's mind, Jonquil Steadman Carter was a perfect, purple unicorn.

"Damn, girl! You sho' 'nuff can hear an ant pissin'

on cotton," he said. He took a bite of the first of two guilty pleasures he allowed himself every day. Had his blood sugar been any higher when he checked it an hour earlier, he would have had to forego the Oreo cookies for another day.

Even more than his beloved granddaughter, diabetes was his closest companion. He knew he needed to keep it in check until the girl either finished college or got married off. Both those circumstances were, he hoped, many years down the road. At his age, he also knew diabetes could become a real problem if he didn't keep an eye on it and behave, especially with sweets, double-especially, sweets like Oreo cookies. Still, they made his taste buds dance, and every day he looked forward to sharing them with Jonny.

"So, what do you think I should write about for my history of Pitts County, Mississippi paper, Poppop?" she asked through a mouthful of cookie.

He feigned thoughtfulness, rubbed his chin, pursed his lips, and looked around from side to side. Finally, he smiled and stared right into Jonquil's wide brown eyes. "I ain't got the foggiest, girl. What near eighty years livin' in this godforsaken patch of dirt and red ants tells me, nothin' much's happened here, and what did happen ain't worth writin' about."

Jonquil frowned, threw her arms out, and looked to the heavens. "Poppop, you are not even trying. I mean, nothing? That's what you got for me? Nothing?"

He finished his second cookie and washed it down

with the rest of his lemonade. "Guess you're going to have to do some a that research stuff you always talkin' about," he said. "'Scuse me, ma'am, but now, I gots to go pee."

Jonny sighed, shrugged her shoulders, and collected her backpack. She walked around the side of the house toward the big, ancient live oak standing by itself sixty feet down the gently sloping back yard. Raymond grabbed the screen door handle, silently promising himself to paint the door next spring, and headed inside.

When he came out of the bathroom, Raymond meandered to the window overlooking the back porch. He saw Jonny looking at her iPad, stretched out on the oversized bench he had built years earlier. It sat directly beneath a low branch of the dying oak. A local arborist told Raymond back in the nineties the tree at that time was at least 250 years old. Jonny had been asking him for three years to hang a swing from the branch. So far it hadn't happened. With nearly forty acres of land leading to Taylor Creek, it seemed there was always something else to do. As it was, it took two days each week in a long-sleeved shirt and a wide-brimmed straw hat on his old John Deere riding mower to keeping the three-quarters of an acre of fescue and weeds behind the house under control during northwest Mississippi's steamy seven-month growing season.

Beyond the mowed grass, the remaining treed

acreage formed a buffer between his property and the ugly, kudzu-draped remains of the once bustling textile mill visible on the far side of Taylor Creek.

It had been a long time since the property around the house stretched almost 245 acres, filled with open stands of forest between forty-acre tracts of soybeans and hay. Raymond thought about how, after Jacinta died, he began sharecropping, then selling off the fertile tracts to help stretch his military pension, Social Security, and the small stipend he received for his time working at the old Taylor mill. He owned the property free and clear. Someday, whatever was left of it would pass along to Jonquil.

The trees started coming down whenever Raymond had need for winter firewood. What he didn't use for himself and his family, he tied into bunches of a dozen split logs and sold from the bed of his pickup truck parked at the end of his driveway up at the pike. When it got to be more than he wanted to do, his son-in-law, Marcus, began the process of clearing the land, tree by tree. At first, he worked directly behind the house, leaving mostly empty lawn and the one old oak. The way the property existed in its present state was all Jonny ever knew.

Raymond watched as Jonny closed her iPad and downed the last of her lemonade. Using her backpack as a pillow, she stretched out on the bench. He smiled. "So, that's what kids call research these days." *Don't*

*you pay no mind to that old tree, Jonny. Nothing there
you need to study on.*

Raymond was watching *Ellen* when Jonny burst into
the house. "May 26, 1960," she announced.

"December 9, 2002," he said back to her.

She smirked. "I know when I was born, Poppop."
She sat down on the sofa and opened her pad again.

"You know, that . . . that date, what'd you say it
was?" he asked.

"May 26, 1960."

"Just a question here, Jonny," he said. "I saw you, um,
researching out under that old dead tree. Now how'd
you come up with some date while you was sleepin'?"

Jonny closed the pad and paced around the small
front room of the bungalow. "Promise you won't laugh,"
she said.

Raymond went on alert. "What you got to say to
me, Jonquil?"

"I dreamed it," she said, avoiding his stare.

He had no idea how to respond. He exhaled. "You
dreamed it," was all he could say. She continued to
walk around the room.

"Actually," she said, "I dreamed the tree told me
that date."

Raymond focused his eyes on the basket of plastic
pinecones and cloth magnolia blossoms in the hearth

of the no longer working fireplace below the TV. "Jonny, would you please get me a bit more lemonade?"

She walked down the hall, into the kitchen. "I must sound like a real dope. A tree talked to me, in a dream."

She brought two glasses into the living room and handed one to Raymond. "I know it sounds dumb, but it's . . . it's what happened." She sat down next to him. "It was clear, clear as us talking to each other right now."

"I was gonna tell you," Raymond said, "I think that might have been the day Senator Kennedy came through this area. He was running for president and—"

"Okay, I'll check that out, but I think there's maybe something else," she said.

He turned and looked at her. "Of course, Jonny. With you, there's always maybe something else," he said, trying not to let emotion slip into his voice or demeanor. "What else that tree say to you in the dream?"

"I know you don't believe me," she said.

"What else, Jonny?"

"'It didn't happen.'"

"What? None of it happened? Is that what you're telling me?"

"No, Poppop," she said. She started tearing up. "Please don't get angry with me."

He placed his glass of lemonade onto a coaster on the coffee table and took her hands in his. "I don't never get angry at you, Jonny, but you gotta know your own self none of this makes any sense."

"The tree said, 'May 26, 1960,' but then it said, 'It didn't happen.' So, I guess what I'm asking is, do you have any idea what . . . maybe . . . didn't happen on that day?"

Raymond knew exactly what did and what didn't happen on May 26, 1960. He was attempting to understand how Jonny came up with something he and at least two other people that were still alive and living in Vosalia had worked very hard to keep secret for over half a century. He played with the collar of the turtleneck he wore under his chambray shirt.

"I'm going upstairs, Poppop." Jonny said. "I need to do homework."

"Okay, honey, you go do some homework," he said. "I'll let you know when your supper's ready."

Jonny closed the door of her room. "That didn't go so well," she muttered, and sat down on the cedar chest at the foot of the bed and looked at the huge poster of Olympic gold medalist Sanya Richards-Ross, which faced Jonny whenever she sat on the chest or put her head on the pillow at the end of a day of school and track practice. Sanya's face had a big smile on it, but there was also a look of hard resolve in her eyes. Jonny always thought Sanya was saying to her, *You may be good girl, but you aren't me.* Jonny always told the poster, "Not yet, but I will be."

No matter how much her grandfather would have

preferred Jonny be Jonquil, a sweet, dainty, anxious-to-please, girly kind of girl, Jonny was who she was. Thrilled to finally be in high school, she immediately tried out and secured a spot on the Pitts Panthers girls' track team, running the 400 meters and the 4x400 meters relay, Sanya's events when she attended a catholic high school in south Florida.

Jonny planned to try out for the girls' basketball team as soon as she was eligible and was already almost two inches taller than Sanya's full grown five feet eight. Dawn Staley might have to be her new role model.

She pulled her notebook out of her backpack and reviewed her history teacher's assignment. It was clear. Write a paper between 500 and 1,000 words on something of historical significance, which occurred in or near Pitts County, Mississippi. The due date was less than three weeks out. What to do this dumb paper on?

"Dumb tree," she said, out loud.

CHAPTER 2

Thursday, October 19

After her classes for the day ended, Jonny asked her coach if she could be excused from track practice. She rode her bike to the Pitts County public library in downtown Vosalia. A worktable filled with other students from school, all boys, noted her arrival.

She used library technology to confirm there was a fire on May 26, 1960, in the historic, converted downtown Vosalia house containing the offices of the *Pitts County Clarion*. The *Clarion* was the small rural county's weekly newspaper and its only news source. Nothing was published for several weeks after the fire.

She could write something about the newspaper fire, but that actually happened. The tree had told her something *didn't* happen on May 26, 1960. "What does that even mean?" she asked out loud.

"Shhhh." The sound came from directly behind her.

"Oh, sorry, Miss Faraday," Jonny whispered.

"Can I help you with something, sweetheart?" The librarian was a nice, older lady that'd taken a mentor-like interest in Jonny.

"I don't know, Miss Faraday. I have an assignment to write something for school about Pitts County history. I'm trying to find out if anything was supposed to happen on May 26, 1960, but actually didn't happen." Jonny wasn't ready to reveal her source regarding the specific date.

"You mean something was scheduled to take place that day but didn't?" Miss Faraday said. She took a seat at the computer and hit a few keys.

"Well," she said, "that was the day of the newspaper fire. Let's look at the newspaper on the day they started publishing again. Maybe something is here."

Jonny moved closer and looked over her shoulder. Surely the newspaper would report on something important that didn't happen, even days or weeks later.

The next edition of the *Pitts County Clarion* came out June 30. There was, of course, major coverage of the fire. Miss Faraday scanned the article.

"The police and fire departments investigated the fire. They believed from the outset it was arson. That's how it turned out." She looked at Jonny. "Do you know—"

"Yes ma'am," Jonny said. "I know what arson means. I watch *Law and Order* sometimes, with my grandfather."

"Seems like they never stop playing that old *Law and Order* show," Miss Faraday said. "Oh, look here."

In addition to comprehensive coverage of the fire and the brief investigation that followed, the June 30 edition carried police blotter reports for the preceding four weeks.

"Let's see if there's anything else here for May 26 . . ."

Jonny leaned in and looked at reports for that Thursday. *Pitts County deputies investigated multiple reports of shots fired on the Pitts Taylor Pike near property owned by Sam Hampton. Deputies were unable to determine the source of the incident.*

"Hmmm," Jonny said. "We live out on the pike, but I don't know about any Sam Hampton out that way."

"This was a long time ago, Jonny," Miss Faraday said. "After so many years, property along the pike has likely changed ownership. Maybe more than once."

"What kind of shots fired incident do you think they were talking about?" Jonny asked.

Miss Faraday took a quick look around the room. "It's hard to know," she said, trying to keep her voice down. "This place . . . Pitts County . . . Vosalia was . . . different back then. It could have been anything from, I don't know, kids up to some mischief to Klan activity . . ."

"I've heard about the Klan, but I don't know much about them, except they didn't like black folks."

"Still around and still don't," Miss Faraday said.

"Maybe you should ask your grandfather. I'm sure he was here around that time."

Jonny collected her books and bag. "Thanks, Miss Faraday. 'Hampton' you said, right? That's my teacher's name. I wonder ..."

Miss Faraday started to walk away but turned back. "Jonny," she said, "you're very bright and very determined. I know you want to make a good grade on this assignment. Maybe you should consider something more ... I don't know ... well known in the history of this area. You might not be aware, but this part of the state has history going back before Mississippi even became a state. There were several Native American tribes here; there were important people from Pitts County involved in the abolitionist movement—"

"I know some of that, Miss Faraday, but I want to see if I can find out why May 26, 1960, was important. There's something about that day that matters."

The librarian walked back to her desk, opened a drawer, and removed a Pitts County telephone directory.

"I see four Hamptons listed in the current phone book. Two of them, Elijah and Jesse, still live out that way. She ran a copy of the page.

"Time for some research," she said, smiling. She handed Jonny the copied page. "Good hunting."

Jonny looked at the names. "Guess I'll start with Jesse Hampton. He's who gave me this assignment."

"Well," the librarian whispered, "that's his son sitting over there with those other boys from school."

Jonny smiled. "I know Todd," she said. "Everyone does. He's cool. Those others . . . I don't know about them."

⚜

"Have you lived here all your life, Poppop?" Jonny asked her grandfather after they finished off the better part of a pot of shrimp, chicken, and Andouille sausage gumbo he'd prepared for their dinner.

"'Cept for my time in the military service," he said. "Born in Delacourt Hospital over in Taylor County on the twenty-first day of July, nineteen and thirty-eight. They didn't birth black babies back then in Pitts County, 'cept if you was born in your house. Why you ask, Jonny?"

"You ever see any Klan stuff around here?"

He set his spoon down in the empty bowl, patted his lips with his napkin, pushed himself away from the table and stood up. "Are we still talking about 1960, Jonny?" Because that was not a good time around here, and I really don't want you digging around in that until you're older and can maybe understand some of those things a little better."

She shot him her best look of exasperation. "How much older I gotta be?"

This time he glared at her. She couldn't tell if he

was angry at her question, at her tone, or if he was just being her grumpy old Poppop.

"Maybe fifty or sixty years old!" he said. He turned and walked out of the dining room.

"You didn't answer my question, Poppop," she shouted at his back.

❧

Friday, October 20

Jonny remained in her seat after the bell rang, ending Jesse Hampton's history class. After the other students left the room, she approached his desk. "Excuse me, Mr. Hampton," she said. "Can I ask you something?"

Mr. Hampton boosted himself onto the front of his desk and regarded her. "Don't you have a class next period, Jonny?"

She shook her head. "No, sir. Track practice today."

"The four hundred, right?"

"That's right," she said, smiling. "Are you following my career?"

He laughed. "You, I am told, are one of the brightest lights on our track team. Now, what can I help you with?"

She told him she was trying to come up with a topic for the history paper he assigned, but she had no intention of telling him about her dream, or the old oak tree, or anything like that. "Did your family ever own property out on Pitts Taylor Pike?"

He nodded. "Still do," he said. "Used to own quite a bit of it. In fact, I believe my late uncle owned the property near where you and your grandfather currently live. My father still owns a sizable piece of land across the pike, up toward Taylor County. We—myself, my wife, and our son, Todd—live in the subdivision near the county line. Why do you ask?"

"Is your father Elijah Hampton?"

"The one and only," he said, smiling.

She wasn't sure how much to say or how much to hold back, but he didn't seem bothered by the question. "I'm trying to find out about something that may or may not have happened somewhere out along that road back in 1960," she said.

"For the Pitts County history assignment?" he asked her.

"Yes sir," she said.

He moved to the other side of his desk and perched on the front corner, directly across from her. "I don't guess I ever said anything to you, Jonquil, but I knew your father and your mother," he said. "Actually, Beth and I—she's my wife—we were at their wedding."

"You were?"

"We were," he said. "Your father and I played football here, for Pitts County High School. We were on the team together for one season. He was a sophomore when I was a senior. And, if I recall correctly, your mother, her name was Tonya, am I right?"

She nodded. "I never knew either of them," she said.

"Oh, I'm sorry. Somehow, I didn't realize that. Of course, you didn't know them. You were just a baby when they passed."

"My grandfather told me about both of them," she said. "Was he any good, at football, I mean?"

Mr. Hampton laughed. "Yes, he was very good, much better than I was. And your mother was very pretty. I think your father introduced her to me after our team beat Taylor in the last game of the season."

They looked at one another. At nearly the same moment, they both said, "Small town."

"That's the truth," he said. "You know, I see a little bit of both of them in you." He smiled. "Is there anything else I can do for you, Jonquil?"

"Do you think you could maybe ask some of your kin who might have been around back then?" she asked.

"Where did you come up with the idea that something, what did you say, 'may or may not have happened' out on the pike some time in 1960?"

"Not some time," she said. "May 26, 1960." As soon as the date left her lips she regretted it. Her teacher cocked his head. His eyes bore into her.

"That exact date?" he asked. "Jonny, what are you thinking 'may or may not' have happened?" She looked down at her feet.

"I don't know," she said. "And that's the truth. I don't know why that particular date flew into my head. But it did. It was the day of the fire at the newspaper, but

I think something else might have happened on that date. And it may have happened out there."

He was silent for a moment, and she avoided eye contact. "Well," he said, finally, "let me do a little research of my own. But, just an idea here . . . maybe it would be good if you thought about going further back."

"Further back?" she asked.

"I mean, further back in history, Jonny. As in, maybe back to the War Between the States. That's the kind of further back I mean. Pitts County has a rich history of connection and involvement in the war. What went on here after the Civil War, even after World War II, unfortunately, isn't all that wonderful." He paused. "The truth is, while I wasn't around back then, my father told me it wasn't a real good time here."

That made three people—her grandfather, Miss Faraday, and now Mr. Hampton—all trying to discourage her from looking too closely at May 26, 1960.

"I'd appreciate that, Mr. Hampton," she said.

He smiled. "Appreciate what, Jonny?"

She smiled at him. "I'd appreciate learning whatever you might discover. Maybe between us we can figure out what happened in Pitts County back in May of 1960."

CHAPTER 3

Friday, October 20

After school, Jonny stopped by the library in Vosalia before heading home. When she arrived, Miss Faraday was talking and laughing with an older woman. Jonny let them finish before approaching the librarian. The old woman turned to leave. When she noticed Jonny, her face softened, and she smiled.

"Excuse me, young lady, but are you Turtle's little granddaughter?" she asked.

"Yes ma'am," Jonny said, smiling at her grandfather's nickname. "I just call him Poppop."

"You resemble your mother. Well, when you see . . . your Poppop, would you please tell him Martha Plemmons sends her best regards?"

"I will, Mrs. Plemmons."

"Thank you, but it is Miss Plemmons, not Mrs."

"Yes ma'am," Jonny said. "I'll tell him."

The old woman pushed a three-wheeled walker outside and headed west on South Street. Jonny was still smiling when Miss Faraday appeared at her side and put her arm around Jonny's shoulder.

"That woman, right there," she said, "is a living history of this town. You know, you should consider a visit with her. She lives around the corner, on Camille Street, maybe five minutes from here."

"She seems nice," Jonny said. "She knows my Pop— my grandfather."

"I'm not surprised. Your grandfather, a few people call him Turtle, I'm not sure why. He's quite well known and, to be honest, quite highly regarded here in Pitts County."

"I asked him about it, the Turtle thing," Jonny said, "but he says it's just something people called him most of his adult life."

Miss Faraday cocked her head at Jonny. "What's on your agenda for today, young lady?"

"I was wondering," Jonny said, "whatever happened with the fire at the newspaper? It was arson, right? That article you showed me said they found out who did it. Is there a way I can get more information about that?"

Miss Faraday shrugged her shoulders. "I'm sure the newspaper would be the best resource for that. Probably you should talk to Jeff Dellinger. He's their archivist. Well, he's a lot of things over there at the *Clarion*. Also, he writes about the history of the area.

He might be a good resource for you beyond just the fire. Let me give him a call and see if he can visit with you."

"Thank you, Miss Faraday," Jonny said and waited while the librarian made the call. After a brief chat with whoever was on the other end, she signaled to Jonny.

"I told him what you're looking for," she said. "He'll probably have whatever they have on the disposition of that incident ready when you get there. You know where they are?"

"I do, over by Greene Street," she said. "Thank you so much, Miss Faraday.

Jonny exited into a cool, sunny fall afternoon and walked the four blocks to where the *Clarion* occupied the corner space of a former furniture store, across the street from Vosalia's community theater.

When Jonny walked in, a man seated in a wheelchair in the lobby looked up. He had a nice smile on his face, along with rimless eyeglasses, long, straight, salt and pepper hair tied back in a small ponytail, and a bushy, silver beard.

"Miss Carter, I presume?" he said.

"Jonquil Carter," she said, "but you can call me Jonny. Are you Mr. Dellinger?" They shook hands.

"Right the first time," he said. "Welcome to the *Pitts County Clarion*. I understand you're interested in the *Clarion* fire back in 1960. Do I understand correctly?"

"Yes sir," she said.

"Please don't call me sir, Jonny. That title was reserved for my father. If he were still living, he'd be almost as old as your grandfather, Mr. Steadman." He smiled at her look of surprise. "Everyone around here knows Raymond Steadman." He handed her a sheaf of papers. "This is everything I could print off in the time it took you to get here," he said. "I'm not sure exactly what it is you're looking for . . ."

"I'm trying to find information about something that either happened, or was supposed to happen, or almost happened but didn't on May 26, 1960," Jonny said. "It should have been reported in the following week's newspaper, but since the building burned down that day nothing was reported for several weeks. The only thing Ms. Faraday could find was about some shooting incident that took place out on the pike, but I haven't found anything more about that, either."

"So," Jeff Dellinger said, "you think if you could find out something more about the fire you could work your way forward or backward from there, right?"

Jonny brightened. "Yes sir, er, that's right, Mr. Dellinger."

He wheeled himself over to the vinyl-covered seats in the lobby reserved for people waiting to talk to him or someone else at the newspaper. Jonny followed and sat down next to where he'd parked himself. "Let's take a look at what we have," he said.

There were perhaps thirty copied pages of newspaper stories about the fire, the two men accused of starting it, and reports about their capture, subsequent trial, and incarceration.

"You can have these," he said, "but the long and short of it is, two local men, Richard Holmes and Arthur Collins, were arrested the day after the fire. They were identified by an anonymous caller who saw them throw a—do you know what a Molotov cocktail is, Jonny?" She shook her head. "It's another term for a bottle filled with gasoline, with a rag soaked in gasoline stuffed into the neck of the bottle, like a wick," Dellinger said. "When someone lights the rag with a match or cigarette lighter, basically what you have is a firebomb."

"Someone saw these two men put a firebomb into the newspaper building?" she asked.

"They didn't put it in the building, they threw it through a window," he said.

"Wow! And someone saw them?"

"That's right. A highly reliable witness. And, the next day, soon as they were brought in for questioning, Collins tried to blame the whole incident on Holmes. Holmes, in turn, blamed the whole incident on Collins. They both tried to implicate Sam Hampton, but that never gained any traction. These two were not the sharpest knives in the drawer, if you know what I mean."

Jonny smiled, then laughed. "That's funny. I like that. Dull, right?"

"Like a sponge. Then, some equally brilliant

character, who somehow stumbled upon a law degree, Davis Barnes was his name, convinced the two of them to plead not guilty so he could make a few more dollars from a trial. Only problem with that strategy was, someone who knew them saw Collins and Holmes do it. Once they realized they were busted, they fired the lawyer, pleaded guilty to arson, and were sentenced by Judge Alvin Long to the state penitentiary down at Parchman Farm."

"Do we know whatever happened to them?" Jonny asked.

"Darcy didn't tell me about your interest in this other than you have a paper to write on something historic that happened in Pitts County," he said. "Are you writing about the fire, or is there something more?"

Jonny stood and began pacing. She turned back and told Jeff Dellinger about the "incident" that took place out on Pitts Taylor Pike and was reported on in the first edition of the newspaper after the fire.

"I'm fourteen years old, Mr. Dellinger, so anything that happened before I was born is history to me," she said. Jonny didn't want to talk about her dream or the oak tree with this man she'd just met. "I really can't explain why that date, May 26, 1960, came into my head, but that is exactly what happened. I'm starting to think the date, the incident out on the pike, whatever that was, and the fire at the newspaper . . . It just feels to me like all these things might be connected. Vosalia is a small town, right? Except for the Civil War and a couple of other things, nothing much really ever happened here."

Jeff Dellinger smiled at her. "So, it's that date you're interested in, right?"

He was nice and he seemed to want to help her. "Yes," she said.

He sighed. "Well, both men are dead, so there's no talking to them about anything," he said. "They served eight years. They were local men. Holmes worked for the county as a maintenance supervisor. Collins worked at the county's motor pool. And Sam Hampton, who may or may not have been involved, left Vosalia a couple of years after the fire. He moved to Florida I believe. I'm not sure if he's still alive, but I don't think he is. All three were part of the local Klan back then . . ."

Jonny's head snapped around. "The Ku Klux Klan?" she asked.

He nodded. "Do you know much about that, Jonny?"

"Just they don't like black people . . ."

"Or Jews, or Catholics, or Mexicans, or anyone not of northern European ancestry, not white, and not Protestant," he said. "Has any of this been helpful? I mean, for the paper you want to write?"

"Honestly, sir, I don't know," she said. "I mean, Mr. Dellinger.

He smiled at her. "If you need anything else, don't hesitate to call me or to come by Jonny."

She thanked him. As she walked to the door, he said, "And, thanks for not asking about the chair."

She turned and slumped her shoulders. "I am so sorry," she said. "I'm just so into this whole history project thing. I'm sorry for not asking."

"No, no, I'm serious," he said. "It's nice when someone sees the person and not just the wheelchair. It was a car accident about six years ago." She walked back and gave him a hug.

"Thanks again."

"You know," he said, "one more thing before you leave. You might want to talk to Erasmus Belvoir."

"The senator?" she asked.

He smiled. "Retired Senator. I know your grandfather knows him. The two of them have been around here since, well, forever. Maybe the actual date won't mean much but, who knows?"

CHAPTER 4

Saturday, October 21

Tommy sat behind the wheel of his father's red Ford F-150, waiting for the girl to leave track practice. Bobby rode shotgun. Fred was stretched out on the back seat.

"There she is," Bobby said. Tommy drove the truck down Edwards Avenue, nearly a hundred yards behind the girl, watching as she walked and then jogged past the Pitts volunteer fire station.

"Once she turns onto the pike, we'll take her," Fred said.

"Remember," Tommy said, "she goes to school with us. Chances are good she knows who we are." He didn't talk much to Fred or even to Bobby, his best friend since Tommy and his family relocated from Hattiesburg to Vosalia, but he did follow Fred's lead when they were out running around together. Bobby chattered constantly, asking questions, making stupid proclamations. Fred was fond of telling Bobby to either quiet down or get lost.

"Why would she know us?" Fred said. "First, she's a freshman and we're juniors. Second, we're white and she's not."

Tommy said, "I know where she's going. I seen her out running on the pike yesterday when I checked to see where she lives."

The girl put distance between them. "Shit, she can run!" Fred said.

"She's on the track team," Bobby said. "Y'know, they can run faster than us, right?"

"They can't outrun an F-150, stupid," Tommy said. He closed the gap between her and the truck. She jogged until the stop sign at the pike. She still hadn't noticed them. She turned, dropped into a ready-set position, and took off sprinting.

"Damn," Bobby said. "I think maybe she can outrun this piece-of-shit truck."

Seeing no police or sheriff's cruiser, Tommy rolled through the stop. He realized she was actually putting distance between herself and the truck. He stepped on the gas. He quickly caught up, then passed her, and added another fifty yards before pulling onto the shoulder where she was running. She caught up just as they got out of the truck.

"You guys offering me a ride?" the girl asked. "That's

nice but—" She stopped when Tommy and Fred put themselves right in her path. She looked at the two of them while Bobby slowly made his way behind her.

"Understand you been asking questions about something happened here a whole long time ago," Fred said. "Why you so interested in some fire from before you or even your mama and daddy was born?"

"Writing a history paper about Pitts County," she said, "not that it's any of your business."

Tommy stepped up close to her and pushed her with a single hand on her shoulder. He liked showing off for Fred. "You need to show some respect," he said. "Know your place, you know?"

She slapped his hand away and stepped forward. She was taller than him. "Know my place? Who do you think you're talking to?"

Fred stepped up and slapped her in the face. "Just find something else to put in your fucking history paper," he said. "Otherwise, things could get very bad for you." She rubbed her cheek and moved to the side so she could see all three of them.

"Just so you jackasses understand, I know you. I know who you are. I know—" Bobby pushed Jonny into Tommy's arms. He held her tight while Fred got up in her face.

"You don't know *shit*, you ugly goddam coon," he said, slapping her face for a second time. "You don't know shit!" Tommy let her go. The three of them showed her their backs and climbed into Tommy's truck. He cranked it up, negotiated a quick U-turn, and rolled down his window.

"I saw y'all in the library, you know?" she said. "I know who you are. All of you a-holes!"

"Listen, Carter," Tommy said, "you're supposed to be one of the smart ones. Don't do nothin' stupid might get you all messed up." He rolled up his window and headed back toward downtown Vosalia.

When Jonny arrived home, she found her grandfather asleep in his chair on the front porch. She decided to keep the incident to herself for the moment. She tiptoed alongside him, took the half-filled cup of lemonade from his hand, and quietly opened and closed the screen door. She went into the kitchen, filled the glass, and took four Oreo cookies from the package in the pantry. Instead of going back through the front door, she slipped onto the back porch, out the screen door, down three steps, and walked to the big oak.

She took her iPad from her backpack and typed a note to herself about the incident with the three boys. She'd memorized the license plate on the red F-150. She typed three names, Tommy Boggs, Bobby Glass, Fred Holmes.

"Holmes," she said aloud. She pulled out the paper copies about the fire Jeff Dellinger had given her. "Arthur Collins and Richard Holmes. I wonder . . ."

She closed her iPad and closed her eyes. Soon, she was sound asleep under the old oak tree.

Despite the cool October temperature, when Jonny woke up, she was perspiring like it was one of those hot, still, August days in northwest Mississippi. She grabbed her iPad and checked the time. She'd been asleep for nearly an hour. She saw her grandfather fussing around in the kitchen.

She pulled some small pieces of the dream she'd just had back from the edge of wherever her dreams typically went when she woke up. She collected her stuff and walked back to the house.

"You enjoy your *research*, Jonquil?" Raymond said to her, smiling as he finished pan-frying four thin pork chops he'd dipped in egg and breaded with cornmeal.

"That smells good, Poppop," she said. "Need any help?"

"You can open a can of those seasoned green beans in the pantry and put 'em on the stove here for a few minutes. That be enough for you tonight, Jonny, couple chops and green beans?"

"Got any cornbread?"

"And if I do?"

"Then that's plenty, Poppop."

She did as he asked. They ate their dinner. She cleaned up the dishes and met him on the front porch.

"What'd you decide to do for that history paper of yours?" he asked.

She struggled with what or how much to tell him. She didn't like to lie, especially to him. He taught her the importance of honesty, even when the truth complicated things.

"Something did happen out here on the pike on May 26, 1960," she said.

"It had to do with some property owned by one of the Hamptons," she said, "Sam Hampton, but I still don't know what it was or who was involved."

"You not gonna let go of this, Jonny?"

"I don't know what I have to let go of, Poppop," she said. "Do you remember the fire at the *Clarion* newspaper?"

He nodded. "Uh-huh. Everyone remembers that," he said. "Started right around that time you talkin' about. Is that part of your history paper?"

"I think so. I mean, it may be connected, but I'm not sure." She decided to approach something she just dreamed about.

"Poppop," she said. Then she hesitated. "You never answered my question the other day about the Klan. Were there lynchings around here back then?" Before he could respond she remembered something else she had for him.

"Oh, sorry, I almost forgot," she said. "I met someone at the library who knows you. Well, seems like everyone 'round here knows you. Her name is Mrs., no, not Mrs., Miss Martha Plemmons. She was in the library same time I was there. She asked for me to tell you hello." Jonquil smiled. "She was nice. Miss Faraday said I should visit with Martha, that she was a living history of this place."

Jonny's Poppop looked away. Hearing Martha Plemmons' name caused his eyes to lose focus. His face changed, ever so slightly. "Yes, I know her. Or, I should say, I did know Martha Plemmons, a long time ago," he said. "And yes, she was nice, very nice, at least back then. I mean I'm sure she's still very nice. I haven't seen her in . . . Hmm. I don't know how long it's been."

Jonny noted his nervousness. Hands on hips, side-long smile on her face, Jonny said, "You know, you should get into town more often, Poppop. She called you Turtle."

He played with the collar of his shirt.

"Why you wear those things, anyway? You wear them even when it's hot. Is that why they call you Turtle? 'Cause you wear those shirts?"

"Been wearing 'em so long," he said, "just a habit, I suppose. But that's enough about Martha Plemmons or about my clothing choices. Why are you asking me about lynchings? Of course, there were lynchings back then. There were lynchings back then all throughout the south." He paused. "Oh, I see. You think maybe whatever might have happened . . . or didn't happen out here back on May 26, 1960, was a lynching?"

"Yes!" she said. "No." She looked at him as if she were in pain. "I don't know, Poppop."

He smiled and chuckled. "Yes . . . no . . . I don't know. Sounds to me, young lady, like you don't know what you know, and you don't know what you don't know. Not a very good history project you got there, Jonquil Carter."

She sank onto the couch, slumped, and looked at him, dejected. "I know," she said. After a moment, they both started laughing.

"You can't put too much stock in messages you get-tin' from some near-dead oak tree while you're asleep, Jonny," he said. "Am I right? Is that where you gettin' all this nonsense?" She nodded.

"You know," she said, "it's funny. I don't remember my dreams when I sleep at night in my room, almost never. But when I fall asleep under that tree, it's like the tree is talking to me. Out loud. This time, apolo-gizing, even."

"An apologizin' tree. 'Cept for your mama, I don't know much about how fourteen-year-old girls think, Jonquil. And I was much younger then, and I had your grandmother to handle most of the work with her. You the only one of those I got, and I got you all by myself. But here's what I do know, Jonny. Trees don't talk and they definitely got nothin' to apologize for."

"It apologized for whatever it did on May 26, 1960," she said. He took in and let out a deep breath. "I know.

It sounds crazy, even to me, but . . . I don't know, Poppop."

Later, in bed, Jonny replayed her conversations with Mr. Hampton, Miss Faraday, and Mr. Dellinger. They all tried to talk her out of doing her project about that date. Then those three boys tried to scare her off. And her grandfather, who lived here back then and should know all about everything, was being no help at all.

Poppop had told Jonny more than once that her mother could be as stubborn as a field mule. That's how he said it: stubborn as a field mule. He told her she, Jonquil, had inherited that not always admirable trait. She had nodded at the truth in the statement.

She resolved to visit Martha Plemmons. She would, if she could, meet with Senator Erasmus Belvoir. They both lived in Pitts County back then, fifty-seven years ago. Maybe they could shed light on whatever happened or didn't happen on May 26, 1960.

CHAPTER 5

Monday, October 23

It was just a two-block walk from South Street to Martha Plemmons' bungalow on Camille Street. Jonny gave a hesitant knock on her front screen door.

"I'll be right there, young lady," a voice said. Miss Plemmons came to the door, pushing the same three-wheeled walker she'd used when Jonny saw her leave the library. She smiled when she saw Jonny standing on the other side of the screen.

"How'd you know it was me?" Jonny asked.

"I didn't," she said. "I just know gentlemen stopped knocking at my door many years ago, and most of the ladies—women—in Vosalia these days are quite a bit younger than I am." She opened the screen door. "Please, come in. Can I offer you some sweet tea?"

Even in old age, and with her infirmities and her uncolored silver hair, Miss Plemmons' eyes remained bright, and her oval face, strong eyebrows, and half-smile presented the portrait of a refined, elegant, southern woman.

Jonny pulled the door open and stepped across the threshold. She found herself in a place she'd never imagined existed before. "You have such a pretty house," Jonny said, softly. "Thank you so much, ma'am. I would love some sweet tea."

The inside of Martha Plemmons' home was finished in dark, polished woods and soft, pastel fabrics. Richly bound rugs covered hardwood floors in deep reds, lush greens, and soft shades of gold. Ornate valences hung over the tops of heavy draperies around the windows. Jonny's eyes took in expensively framed, original oil paintings on the walls. A magnificent black Steinway baby grand piano, polished to a mirror like finish, sat regally alongside a wall of built-in shelves. Those shelves contained, in Jonny's eyes, hundreds of books.

"Please, Jonquil," Miss Plemmons said, "sit here." She patted a place next to her on a sofa upholstered in pale-yellow silk damask fabric. Jonny tried sitting without actually touching it. "It's a sofa, darling. It's supposed to be sat upon."

Jonny sat and turned to face her gracious hostess. "I'm sorry to come calling without an appointment, Miss Plemmons," she said.

"Oh, I am such a terrible hostess," Miss Plemmons said, lifting herself off the sofa. "Tea!" She moved slowly into the kitchen. Jonny could hear the refrigerator door open and then close. "Jonquil!" she called. "Could you please come in here and carry these glasses? I need at least one of my hands for this infernal walking machine!"

Martha Plemmons' kitchen was similar to the one in the house where Jonny and her grandfather lived, in that it was more up to date than the rest of the home. Jonny collected a wood tray carrying two glasses filled with ice and sweet tea and followed Martha to the living room.

"Please place mine over here," Martha said, pointing to a ceramic coaster atop a dark walnut pie table to the side of the sofa where they were sitting. "You may place yours where it is most comfortable for you to reach, either on the tea table or on the table over there," she said, pointing to an identical pie table on the other side of the sofa. "And please, if you would, use a coaster." Jonny placed her glass on a cork-bottomed coaster atop the tea table.

Jonny couldn't help but wonder if a fine, white, southern lady, like Miss Martha Plemmons, and a young black girl, like herself, would have been able to share sweet tea in the beautiful front room of a fancy old house on Camille Street in downtown Vosalia, Mississippi, on May 26, 1960.

"I'm so delighted you've come to visit, Jonquil," Martha Plemmons said. "I am not quite certain why, but I had the feeling when I saw you at the library it wouldn't be the last time we chatted with each other. Now, before anything else, please tell me how your grandfather is getting on these days?"

Jonny smiled. "He's fine," she said. "Cranky, sometimes, but mostly he's doing fine, Miss Plemmons. Do you know him well? When I told him I saw you, he said you were a very nice person."

Martha's eyes misted. Her cheeks flushed just a bit, and her breathing turned slightly shallow. She took a sip from her glass of tea.

"Your grandfather and I knew one another for a very short period of time, many, many years ago, Jonquil. And, unfortunately, we haven't been in each other's company for . . . heavens, I couldn't even guess how long it has been, even in a town as small and insular as Vosalia," she said. "But please, please tell Turtle that I continue to hold him in the very highest regard, and that I look forward to when we can finally spend some time together and catch up on all that has passed."

She looked away for a moment before turning back to her guest. "Jonquil is such a lovely name," she said. "And such a rare name."

"I know," Jonny said, smiling. "For a long time, I didn't like my name."

"Oh, darling," Martha said. "I don't know a girl or even a boy, for that matter, who, at one time or another, didn't wish they were given some other name, any other name, except the one with which they ultimately got stuck."

"I know," Jonny said. "At least she didn't name me Narcissus."

Martha smiled. "Oh, heavens yes! Then you would have had to be called . . . Narcy?" They both laughed. This led to a brief, uneasy silence.

Before Jonny could ask the question she'd come to ask, Miss Plemmons spoke. "You know"—her eyes roamed around the room, settling anywhere but on Jonny— "your grandfather and I were . . . aware of one another when it wasn't considered very proper for a young black man to even talk to a young white woman." She turned to Jonny. "You didn't know your grandmother Jacinta, did you?"

Jonny took a sip of her tea. "No, Miss Plemmons, I didn't," she said. "I didn't know my grandmother or my mother or my father or my father's people. My grandfather is the only blood family I've ever known."

Martha put her hand on Jonny's and looked deep into her eyes. Jonny noticed the old lady was close to tears.

"I knew your mother, Tonya, and I met your father, Marcus, at their wedding," she said. "That's where I also met your grandmother, Jacinta. She was a lovely and most remarkable woman. I'm sure Turtle has . . . I really must stop calling him that, shouldn't I? I'm sure Raymond has told you all about all of them. But perhaps it's important that you hear from me ... or someone like me . . . these were all fine, fine people. You come from exceptionally good stock, very fine people, indeed, Jonquil."

Her grandfather had, at different times, let Jonny know as much as he possibly could about her relatives. She'd seen pictures of her parents and grandparents, heard stories, and met friends of her grandfather's, who shared more pictures and more stories. She'd gotten small bits of what life was like for her relatives when they were young. Jonny believed she did come from good people even though their neighbors and others didn't necessarily treat them like they were good people or, sometimes, even like they were people at all, for that matter.

Jonny had her own experiences with what she thought of as "the whole white-black thing," and she believed some of those ideas and notions probably would not ever entirely disappear. For whatever reason, she didn't spend a lot of time thinking about race.

"Thank you, Miss Plemmons," she said. "I do appreciate your words and yes, it is important." She took in a deep breath. Martha squeezed her hand.

"I know you came here for a reason, Jonquil," she said. "But before we get to that, would you please do something for me?"

"Of course, Miss Plemmons."

"Good. Would you please stop referring to me as

Miss Plemmons? I'm told we are both living in the twenty-first century. My name is Martha. My friends, the few who are still alive, call me Martha. And I do so hope we are, and always will be very good friends."

Jonny smiled. "I will, Miss—I will, Martha," she said. "Please call me Jonny. That's what my friends call me. But if we're ever around my Poppop, it'll be Miss Plemmons."

They reached for one another's hands and looked deeply into each other's eyes, friends.

"Now, Jonny," Martha said, "let's get down to business. I think I know, but what have you come here today to ask me?"

Jonny began by explaining she had a paper to write for Mr. Hampton's history class, and it had to focus on Pitts County, Mississippi.

"Is that Elijah Hampton's son?" Martha asked.

"Yes, it is," she said. "I can't really explain exactly why, but I'm looking at the time period around the newspaper fire."

Martha nodded and gave a benign smile, but she said, "Okay. Those were very turbulent and contentious times, Jonquil."

Mr. Dellinger had told Jonny it was a good tactic to listen to the person you're interviewing and to keep your questions to the "how" and the "why" of things. "I've heard that from several people," Jonny said. "Why were those times so bad in Pitts County?"

"There are events in life that serve as signposts, Jonny," Martha said. "You're talking about—let me see, May of 1960, am I correct?"

"Yes, ma'am, uh, Martha."

"Okay. Let's begin with something that happened approximately six years before the fire at the newspaper. It didn't happen here, per se, but it had ramifications everywhere."

Martha shared a series of anecdotes regarding life in Pitts County in the contentious years following the US Supreme Court's decision in *Brown v. Board of Education* in 1954. Jonny had already learned in school, in Mr. Hampton's history class, in fact, about the ruling ending legal segregation in public schools. Martha explained how it effectively reversed almost sixty years of what was called "separate but equal" status handed down in another Supreme Court decision, *Plessey v. Ferguson*, which dated all the way back to 1896.

"You must understand, Jonquil," Martha said, "most people in the south and many in the north, for that matter, were quite content with the status quo. 'Separate but equal' meant … separate, and that's what most white people wanted regarding Negroes attending schools."

Jonquil instinctively recoiled at the sound of the word, "Negroes."

"I know," Martha said. "Today, people of color are referred to as black or African American, but for some, there are problems with these words as well. Language is typically a complicating factor in almost any conversation involving race."

Jonny never had a candid dialogue of this nature with anyone before, including her grandfather. Here, a woman she'd just met was speaking to her as if she – Jonny – were an adult, a peer.

"You know, Jonquil," Martha said, "I think it's fair to say, the decision in 1954 by the Supreme Court ending legal segregation is, at least in part, responsible for much of the racial discord that exists in our country, even today."

"Miss Plemmons . . . Martha . . . why did this thing, this *Brown v. Board of Education*, you called it, cause so much trouble?"

"Some may disagree, but the Civil War was fought over the issue of slavery," Martha said. "You haven't studied this?"

"Oh, we have, but it sometimes causes arguments in class when we talk about it."

Martha nodded her head. "I'm not at all surprised," she said. "Race is something very difficult for some people to discuss. That's because it's an emotional issue." She looked into Jonquil's eyes. "*Plessey v. Ferguson* basically affirmed the same resources invested in each white student's education must be invested in each black student's education, but also affirmed the two didn't have to attend the same actual school. *Brown v. Board of Education* reversed the whole 'separate but equal' idea and said black children and white children could, indeed should, attend the same schools. You understand the difference here, don't you?"

Jonny took a moment to digest what Martha had explained to her. "I think I do," she said. "But that was such a long time ago. Is that the reason some of the white kids even now don't like black people?" Martha placed her hands in her lap, exhaled, and turned to face Jonny.

"I was taught, as a child, Jonquil, black people were inferior and dangerous and not anything like white people. As a child. It took years for me to learn first-hand, the fundamental lie that I and almost all my contemporaries were brought up to believe."

Jonny had no idea what to say. She saw the tears on Martha Clemmons's face. She took hold of Martha's hands and smiled at her.

"Your grandfather . . . I'm sorry, sweetheart," Martha said, "there's so much, about that time in history, about how people were brought up to believe and to think, especially here, in the south." She asked Jonny to please get her a tissue from the bathroom down the hall.

"Thank you, Jonquil," she said. She dabbed at her eyes, blew her nose, and put the tissue into a pocket of her floral-print housedress.

"So, it's always been like this," Jonny said.

"And I fear, Jonquil, to some lesser or greater degree, it will always be with us."

Jonny stood and began pacing, forming something in her brain. "Why? What's wrong with people?"

Martha smiled. "It's taken me a long lifetime, and I still haven't figured out why some people think what they think, say what they say, do what they do, and are how they are," she said. "I think it comes down to something quite simple. Things like this usually do. People fear what they don't understand, and they tend to hate what and whom they fear. What helps it to change, what helped change it for me, at least, was meeting Raymond Steadman back then. Your grandfather helped me understand he was just a human being, same as I was. Yes, our skin color was not the same, but deep down, on the inside, beneath the skin, in our hearts, where it counts, we both were human beings. Just people.

"Up until the *Clarion* fire of May 26, 1960, I was like most of my peers. I came from inherited wealth and grew up entitled—privileged, one might say. Unlike most of my friends, I always behaved in a polite and respectful manner toward what were then referred to as 'colored people' and never shied from interacting with any of them, no matter their station.

"When I met your grandfather, I had an epiphany: people were people, and there was no reason to feel either inferior or superior to anyone, regardless of the color of their skin. I was drawn to Raymond almost from the moment we met.

"After two racists, members in good standing of the Pitts County chapter of the Ku Klux Klan, firebombed the newspaper office, I became what they now call radicalized. I started paying attention to the civil rights movement, which was working its way through the American south and was slowly gaining traction on some college campuses, and in some cities. My parents were concerned for my safety but encouraged me to follow my Christian heart. I worked for the election of Erasmus Belvoir to the Mississippi legislature and, years later, to the state senate. I worked on other political campaigns as well. I considered running for public office myself once but chose instead to work in the trenches for both my fellow human beings and for the causes of social justice that I had come to hold dear, such as volunteering in the Pitts County food pantry and helping to register voters, mostly among the poor and minority communities.

"You'd never know it today, but back then many of the young white men in the area thought I looked like Vivien Leigh in *Gone with the Wind*, but they kept their distance due to what their families considered my 'inappropriate' or 'unconventional' politics." They both paused to take sips of tea.

"The revolution in national affairs during the 1960s—the women's movement, opposition to the Vietnam War, and the march toward civil and voting rights—led me three hours down I-55 to Jackson. I stayed there for almost ten years, working eight of those for Erasmus Belvoir. I also volunteered to work on a variety of progressive social justice initiatives, including capital punishment, nutrition assistance, infant mortality, and women's reproductive rights. Through it all I remained deeply committed to my Methodist faith, attending worship services, and often employing biblical references to connect my faith to a social cause. This particularly frustrated, even infuriated, the haters.

"After Richard Nixon resigned the presidency and the Vietnam War ended, I came home to Vosalia. I was left this house and a moderate inheritance when my parents died. I remained close with Erasmus Belvoir, and I kept in touch with your grandfather after he retired from the army until he married Jacinta, and they'd brought your mother into the world. I attended both Jacinta's and Tonya's funerals but otherwise chose to not be involved in your and Raymond's lives. Until this moment, that has been a singular regret."

After her visit, Jonny's head spun like the electric ceiling fan in Miss Plemmons' kitchen. Even though she didn't learn much in the way of specifics regarding what did or didn't happen on May 26, 1960, other than the newspaper fire, her conversation with Martha Plemmons was an honors-level course on life in the south, as she often put it, "back in the day." Her grandfather used the same term when he was talking about things from the past he didn't really want to talk about.

Jonny understood, perhaps more than someone her age should, about the challenges that existed between blacks and whites "back in the day." *Heck, in my case,* she thought, *"back in the day" was just a couple days ago!*

Chapter 6

Tuesday, October 24

"Please, Poppop, please, please, please?" Jonny begged. Raymond couldn't decide whether to be angry with his granddaughter or laugh out loud.

"Jonny," he said, "let me explain something to you, for maybe the fiftieth dang time. I am seventy-nine years old. I haven't driven on an interstate highway since you was born. That old truck out there has as much chance of making it to either Memphis or Oxford as a three-legged mule. This. Is. Not. Going. To. Happen. Do you understand?"

Jonny was determined. Unyielding. Stubborn, one might say, as a field mule.

"I checked, Poppop, and neither the Memphis newspaper nor the one in Oxford has stuff on their websites that goes back to 1960. I need to find out what . . . didn't happen, I guess, on May 26, 1960 for this project. If I don't, I'll fail!"

Raymond decided on the laughter approach. He knew it would make her even crazier, but he could never get angry when she went all teenage drama queen on him. "Jonny," he said, smiling, "we both know that isn't true. Now, I'm gonna call your teacher, Mr. Hampton. I'm gonna call him and—"

"No! No! You can't do that."

"What you mean, I can't do that. Of course I can do that."

She was pacing the small living room. With those long legs it took her about four strides to get from one wall to the other.

"Have you even tried calling either of these newspapers?"

"No," she said. "I have to see it for myself, with my own eyes."

He sat on the sofa and made a show of ruminating on her problem. He stroked his chin, pursed his lips, nodded, and then shook his head. It had the desired effect. She broke out laughing.

"What are you doing, old man?" she asked, planting herself next to him.

"I," he said, feigning gravitas, "am cogitating."

"Cogitating? Is that, like, digesting your breakfast?" He looked at her with his best stern expression.

"I'm thinkin'," he said.

She looked at him for another moment. "Well," she

said, getting to her feet, "don't hurt yourself. I'm going to go and see Mr. Belvoir."

"Erasmus Belvoir?" he asked.

"Senator Erasmus Belvoir himself," she said.

He stood up. "I'll come with you," he said. "I'll even drive you. It's much closer than either Memphis or Oxford."

"I know that," she said, "but I'd rather speak to him myself, if that's okay."

"You afraid I'll say or do something to embarrass you"

"I do not plan to tell him how I came to be interested in that specific date, okay Poppop?"

"You know, I just had an idea," he said. She cocked her head to one side. "Why don't you take another nap down by that old talkin' tree? Maybe it'll tell you what you need to—" He broke out laughing and put his hands up defensively when she grabbed a pillow from the sofa to throw at him.

"It's not funny, Poppop," she said. Then, she got serious.

"You don't want me looking at that date, May 26, 1960, right?"

He stared at her.

"Mr. Hampton doesn't want me looking at that date. Ms. Faraday, the librarian, doesn't want me looking at that date. Miss Plemmons don't—"

"You talked to Martha Plemmons?"

"I did, and you were right, she is a very nice lady.

Has a beautiful house, but she doesn't want me looking at that date. Mr. Dellinger—"

"She have anything else to say to you?"

"We talked for three hours on Saturday, Poppop. She told me a lot. Now, Mr. Dellinger at the newspaper, he doesn't want me looking at that date. You know what all that tells me?"

He took both her hands in his. "You a big girl but still very young, Jonny," he said, softly. "You don't need to visit places the whole world seems to not want you to visit. You hear what I'm sayin'?"

"I hear you." She sat down, crossed her ankles, crossed her arms over her chest, looked at him, and smiled. "What happened on May 26, 1960, Poppop?"

He redid his whole cogitating exercise. "I can't possibly tell you what happened on one specific day more than half a dang century ago, Jonquil," he said.

She communicated her disbelief by uncrossing and then recrossing her arms.

"Has it occurred to you, young lady," he said, "that if all those people you just named, not to mention your own flesh and blood grandfather who loves you, are encouraging you to forget some date you heard in some kind of dream, from a conversation with a near-dead tree, and focus your history paper on something else, maybe, just maybe, you ought to think about doing that?" He knew he'd wasted his words when she stared at him sternly and then smiled.

"It is precisely because everyone's trying to talk me

out of it, without anyone telling me why they're trying to talk me out of it, that I believe I need to keep looking into it." She recrossed her arms, planted that stern frown on her beautiful, childlike face, and stared at him.

Raymond sighed, shook his head, and then threw his hands up in surrender. "I'm tired, Jonny. Go on. Go see Senator Belvoir."

She picked up her backpack, checked to make sure her iPad was inside, zipped it, and threw it over her shoulder. She walked over, kissed him on his forehead, and left.

He watched her ride her bike down the long driveway toward the pike. When she was out of sight, he pushed himself to his feet, walked to the small table where the telephone sat, and opened the drawer where they kept the remote control to the television. He removed a small red leather-bound book. He opened it, found the number he was looking for, and punched it into the house phone. After three rings, a tired voice answered.

"Been a long time, Turtle," he said.

"How you know it was me?"

"I got that thing on my phone, tells me who's calling."

"Hmmm. Wonder if I got that."

"Been a long time, Turtle."

There was a silence on the line.

"You still there, Turtle?"

"Still here, Elijah. Still here. Now, could you please come by for a few minutes? You and me? We need to talk."

Jonquil's nerves were on edge as she rode to see former Mississippi state senator Erasmus Belvoir. She recalled the day, when she was seven years old; the senator came to Vosalia and announced his impending retirement from state politics. He said he would be returning to the private practice of law in Pitts County.

He had spoken without a microphone to the fifty or so people assembled on South Street. They stood across from the building that used to house the all-black K-12 school he'd been graduated from almost fifty-five years earlier. They cheered when they heard the man locals referred to as Rasmus tell them he would be coming home. A few white folks, as Jonny recalled, shook their heads, and walked away. Her grandfather told her at the time not to pay it any mind. "Some things don't never change, Jonny, no matter how much time passes."

When she got where she was going, she locked her bike onto a stop sign on South Street at the corner of Folsom. As she approached the wooden door that opened onto a staircase leading up to his second-floor suite of rooms, she recalled the senator had pointed to his left when he made the announcement.

"Now y'all won't have to travel all the way to Jackson any longer to get assistance, should you ever require it," he'd said at the time. "My law office is going to be right there on South Street, between Jepson's Furniture Store and Miz Grayson's art gallery. Well, the entrance will be right there. It's eighteen steps up to the actual office."

Jonny opened the door between Jepson's and the pet supplies store, Raising Cats and Dogs. It opened after Miss Grayson passed away. As quietly as was possible, she climbed the eighteen steps to the landing, walked to the frosted glass door marked Erasmus J. Belvoir, Esquire, Attorney at Law, and knocked three times.

"Door's open." It was that familiar baritone known well to the citizens of Pitts County. Jonny opened the door and stepped inside.

"Senator?" she asked.

"Nope," he said, rising behind a cluttered desk. "Not for a while now. My, Miz Carter, but you have grown into a downright beautiful young woman, and tall, too. Look at you! Please, come inside."

In addition to his powerful voice, Erasmus Belvoir presented an imposing physical figure. He was a large man, tall, with a broad chest. He wore his steel-gray hair close to his scalp. The man rarely was seen in public wearing anything but a dark blue or gray pinstriped suit, a blue or white striped, polished cotton shirt, and a silk tie appropriate to the occasion. His shoes were always shined to a high gloss and, when he shook hands with someone, he always rotated his wrist, so his hand was on top.

Jonny wondered if her oversized purple T-shirt featuring a growling gold panther over a pair of jeans that were already torn when she bought them was a fitting look. She walked inside and sat in one of two black leather wingback chairs planted in front of a large, ornate, and cluttered desk.

"You may, for a few years, call me *Mister* Belvoir," he said, "or counselor, if you wish. When you enroll in Ole Miss or Memphis or Alcorn or MSU, at that time, if I'm still here and if you so desire, then you may call me Rasmus like most everyone else around here does." He moved from behind his desk and sat in the other chair. "Now tell me, how's that cranky old man you live with these days?"

Jonny smiled. "He's good. He's a little cranky with me right now."

He asked about her academics, her athletics, and her own health before they settled down to discuss the business at hand.

"Now you told me over the phone that you had some questions about something that happened around here nearly twenty years before your parents were even born," he said. "Have I got that right?"

Once again, Jonny struggled to avoid, at all costs, the whole tree-dream aspect of her inquiry. "We've been assigned to write a paper on something historical that happened in Pitts County," she said. "I'm interested in the time around the end of May in 1960."

"Hmmm," he said. "May of 1960 is a pretty specific time, Miss Carter. May I call you Jonquil?"

"Jonquil's fine," she said, "or you can just call me Jonny like everyone else."

"I was finishing up my second year at Alcorn in May of 1960, Jonny," he said. "Those were problematic times pretty much everywhere, but especially in the deep south and especially for us black folks. Not sure how much I can help you."

Jonny let her eyes roam the walls of his office. They were lined with plaques, certificates of appreciation, and photographs of him with important people, black and white. He had a beautiful onyx bust of Martin Luther King. Interspersed were pictures of him with everyone from Jimmy Carter to Barack Obama and a bunch of other people she didn't know, although she recognized Eli Manning. She remembered hearing he was the first of his family to go to high school. Despite his never having attended the University of Mississippi in Oxford, an Ole Miss blue and white banner hung over the door to his office.

"Why is that up there?" she asked, pointing to the banner. "You went to Alcorn, right?"

"I did," he said. He walked over to the wall with the pictures and took one down. "This man, when he was much younger, was actually the man who helped integrate the University of Mississippi," he said. "That was in 1962, when I was on my way to law school at Howard in Washington, DC. Before James Meredith, Ole Miss didn't take black students."

"How come the banner?" she asked.

He replaced the picture, though for a moment, and nodded his head. "This is all kind of ancient history, but I have what's referred to as a symbiotic relationship with Ole Miss," he said. Jonny grabbed for her iPad. He gave her a moment to look up the word.

"I joined the legislature back in 1978," he said. "The Republicans had gerrymandered the heck out of the state but carved out a couple of districts that would support black candidates. Mine was one of those districts."

Her frown made him smile. He explained that gerrymandering was a tactic the party in control of the legislative branch of government often used to favor themselves at the expense of the opposition party's candidates, especially for Congress. He also told her there were court cases all over America trying to get those gerrymandered districts redrawn more fairly.

"Then," he went on, "in 1980, when Mississippi finally got a governor who wasn't still living in the Jim Crow south, I got an invitation from someone in his office to help put together a class at the university in Oxford—that's where he went to college—on Reconstruction political history up until the present. I taught the class for about three years myself before turning it over to someone who could take it to the next level."

Jonny wasn't quite glazed over, but she had a few questions.

"I don't want to get too off track. I'll talk to you some other time about the Jim Crow south and all that stuff," he said. "And there's still a long way for Ole Miss to go before they join this century—the name of their football team, for example: Rebels—but there are people there working on changing things for the better. Things like that don't happen all at one time."

Jonny watched as Rasmus put James Meredith's picture back where it belonged. He took a moment and then returned to his seat. She continued looking at all the man's memories. She noted only one family picture; Senator Belvoir had never married and had no children. The cap and gown picture, of him standing with two serious people who, Jonny guessed, must have been his parents, in an ornate eight-by-ten-inch frame occupied a special place, alone, on the credenza behind his desk.

"A penny or two for your thoughts, Jonquil?" he asked, smiling at her.

"You know all these people," she said. "You've had a very interesting life."

He broadened his smile. "Well," he said, "I hope I can add a picture of you in cap and gown when you graduate college in, let me see, another seven, eight years?"

"Oh," she said, "there's a long way to go for that, Mr. Belvoir. So, nothing about the end of May in 1960, huh?"

He sighed. "That would have been around the time of the fire at the *Clarion*, correct?" he asked. "Is that what you're talking about?"

It was Jonny's turn to sigh. "That happened right around that time, but I was hoping for something else that might have happened or was supposed to happen but didn't, or . . . Do you recall anything maybe about a lynching that might have . . ."

His face went quickly from relaxed to on alert, serious. He sat straight up in his chair. "Is there something specific you want to ask about, Miss Carter?"

His change of tone and sudden formal demeanor caught Jonny off guard. She made a decision. "I don't know, senator," she said. "I'm sorry if I've wasted your time. I have done as much research as I know how to do, at school, at the library, with my grandfather, my teacher, with Miss Plemmons . . ."

"You talked to Martha Plemmons?" he asked. "She's been around Vosalia longer than most everyone except maybe that old rascal you live with." He paused for a moment. "You know, his father, that would be your great-grandfather, probably acquired that house you're living in and that land sometime soon after . . . It would have had to be sometime after 1962. I think Raymond might have been overseas in the army . . . No . . . When was your grandfather born?"

She felt a surge of new energy. The word Mr. Belvoir had used was "acquired." She always assumed the land had been in the family forever, and Poppop never said otherwise. It wasn't something they'd ever talked about.

"He was born in 1938, Mr. Belvoir," she said. "July 21."

The Senator did some quick calculations in his head and on his hands.

"If I recall correctly, Raymond's father got title to the property out on the pike where you live sometime in 1962 or maybe early '63. It was while I was home from a break just before heading to Howard Law School." He searched the room, trying to find a thought. "I'm pretty sure it was around the same time Sam Hampton left town."

"Sam Hampton?" she asked.

He shook his head. "One of the last of his kind around here," he said. For a moment, Erasmus Belvoir lost himself in some retrieved memory. "Well, maybe not the last, but he was definitely one of the worst." She looked at him unemotionally, hoping he'd continue down whatever road he was traveling.

"You're still awfully young to have to know some of the racist history of this part of the world, Jonquil," he said. "You know, there are things people can hide about themselves, but skin color isn't one of them. Do you understand what I mean?"

She nodded. "I think so."

He thought for a moment. "You know, what am I talking about? You are never too young to know how the real world works when you're in the minority and living in a place where prejudice is a way of life."

He launched into a long, sometimes disjointed litany of incidents involving things that angry white people had said and done to mostly law-abiding black people back before the civil rights era and even since. When he finished it was with an apology and an admonishment.

"I'm sorry, Jonquil—Jonny," he said, standing up and moving back behind his desk. It was a signal she correctly interpreted to mean their time together was coming to a close. "I shouldn't have filled your head with a bunch of stuff that didn't necessarily either answer your question or tell you anything new, other than make you upset. However, as I said earlier, that time, back in the early 1960s, was very difficult round here. It's gotten better, to be sure, but there are still people who don't like the way things are, who wave those Stars and Bars, and who actually believe that they are better simply because they are white, and we are not."

Jonny smiled. "I'm really just trying to write a good paper for Mr. Hampton's history class."

"That's Jesse, right? Elijah's son?"

"Yes sir."

"You've talked to him?"

She collected her notebook and backpack. "Yes, I did," she said. "He's trying to get me off this, just like

Miss Plemmons; just like Ms. Faraday, the librarian; just like my grandfather. Seems like no one wants me to know what did or didn't happen back then."

He came back around his desk and opened his arms. She stepped into his hug.

"I'm not going to try to talk you out of anything, Jonny," he said. "Not sure I could, even if I wanted to. You come from a long line of stubborn people. But take a hard look at that fire at the newspaper. It didn't just happen for no reason, you know?"

Jonny thanked the retired state senator and turned to leave.

"Miss Carter," he said. She turned to face him. "I wonder if your grandfather would mind if I came by a little later—around five or so—and picked you up. There's a town council meeting this evening you might find illuminating."

Jonny smiled. "I don't think he'd mind at all, Mr. Belvoir," she said. "I'll just tell him we have a date!"

He gifted her with a broad, toothy smile. "It's a date, then!"

She thanked him again and left. She went down the staircase and out onto South Street, thinking about what he'd said. Maybe she should spend some more time with Mr. Dellinger over at the newspaper. She unlocked her bicycle from the stop sign at the corner of South Street and Folsom Avenue and headed home to get ready for her "date" with retired state senator Erasmus J. Belvoir.

Chapter 7

The two old men walked past the sad old oak without stopping. "You and your son-in-law cut down so many of these trees. Why is that ugly one over there still standing?" Elijah Hampton asked.

"Dyin' all by its own self," Raymond said. "Like us, I guess. 'Sides, in some manner of speaking, that damn tree is a part of all this nonsense goin' on."

They left the open space behind the house and followed a narrow path through an area wooded with poplars, oaks, a few scraggly pines, and some sweet gums. There was a carpet of leaves accumulated from decades of winters. They ended up near the edge of Taylor Creek.

"Let me see if I got this straight now," Elijah said, "your granddaughter—oh by the way, my son, and my grandson, say she's not only a very good student but she's also quite the athlete."

Raymond nodded. "She is. Thank you for sayin' so. You started sayin' something else," he said.

"I did. Your granddaughter, Jonquil, right? Jonquil fell sleeping under that old oak back there, and when she woke up, she said, 'May 26, 1960.' I got that right?" Elijah asked.

Raymond nodded again. "'May 26, 1960,' and 'It didn't happen.' Then, a couple days later, she falls asleep again, wakes up, comes back to the house, and asks me about lynchings and tells me the tree says that it's sorry."

They passed through the edge of the woods where, off to the right, they could see the creek and the remains of the abandoned mill on the other side. The stone fireplace, another remnant from decades past, was still visible behind them.

"She wants to write her history paper about whatever happened . . . or whatever didn't happen"— Raymond said, looking directly into Elijah Hampton's eyes— "on that day, specifically. I think now she's focusing more on the fire at the newspaper, but both of us knows where that stuff ends up."

Elijah counted off on his left hand and then switched to his right.

"I guess we managed to mostly keep a lid on those unfortunate events for better part of a half century," he said. "You say she talked to Martha Plemmons?"

Raymond again nodded his head. "She's with

Erasmus right now," he said, and checked the time on his wristwatch. "Uh, oh. She's probably on her way. You best be skedaddling, my friend. I don't want to have to explain you being here to her right now."

They walked back to the house. Elijah climbed into his truck. "You know," he said, "I guess I could tell Jesse to just tell Jonquil that she needs to write about something else, or he'll give her an F on her paper."

"Yeah, I know you could," Raymond said, "but I don't want him to do that, Elijah. She needs to either see this through or move away from it on her own."

"You still wearing those ugly shirts I see," Elijah said, smiling.

Raymond ignored Elijah's comment. "Maybe it's time we let this play out, once and for all," he said.

Elijah looked at him, smiled, and nodded. "Yep, that might be fun." He tipped his US Army veteran ball cap, started the old Ford truck, and headed down the long gravel drive to the Pitts Taylor Pike. Raymond watched him leave and then stayed where he was until, minutes later, Jonny pedaled her bike onto the driveway and up to the house.

"Who was that?" she asked.

"Old friend," he said. "Very old. Even older than me. You hungry?"

"Starving," she said, parking the bike near the handrail leading up to the porch. "Senator . . . 'scuse me, Mister Counselor Belvoir sends his regards."

Raymond snorted. "Come on in and tell me what that old gasbag had to say."

"Well, he said he'd like to pick me up later and take me with him to a town council meeting. You good with that?"

"Just met the man and he's taking you to a meeting?" he asked, incredulous. "Well, I guess that's okay. Every time those council folks get together nothin' good happens."

She smiled at him. "Maybe we can do dinner a little early then?"

"Gotta disrupt the whole universe for Erasmus Belvoir," he said.

"So," she said, smiling. "You got old friends, huh? Older than you? I didn't think anyone was older than you."

"Well, then I guess you ain't as smart as you think you are, Miss Carter."

Raymond fried a few slices of bologna for sandwiches, with slices of cheddar and American cheese. Jonny toasted four slices of thick, Texas-sized sourdough bread. She slathered on butter and mayonnaise and put the bread on plates along with potato chips and thick slices from a big bright-red beefsteak tomato picked a day earlier from the container garden Raymond tended behind the house.

"I'm going to try and see Mr. Dellinger at his office tomorrow," she said. "I think I'm going to write my paper about the fire at the newspaper. It happened on that day, May 26, 1960."

Raymond finished chewing a mouthful of what he knew was unhealthy goodness, passed down from his own mother, before speaking.

"Time between end of the war and when they signed the Civil Rights Act into law was a hard time here in the south and especially here, in northwestern Mississippi," he said. "I can't believe there isn't something more interesting that happened here before the war." Before she could put the exasperated look on her face into words, he went on. "I guess writing about something that happened, I mean actually happened, though, is better than writing about something that was supposed to happen but didn't."

She looked at him with her head cocked to one side but said nothing. She finished her sandwich and tomato and potato chips, rinsed her plate, put it in the dishwasher, and left the kitchen. At the staircase she turned and looked back. She waved an index finger at him.

"One of these days, you and I are going to have a conversation about some things, Mr. Raymond the Turtle Steadman. I promise you that. Now you go eat your two Oreos, old man." She smiled at him and walked up the stairs.

Raymond and Jonny were on the front porch when Rasmus pulled up in his Lincoln Town Car. He began talking as soon as he wrangled himself out of the front seat.

"I think it's important for young people to get a taste of civics in action," he said. "And I mean 'in action' in both ways. Two words, and one word."

Raymond nodded. "Good to see you, Mr. Belvoir," he said. "Just make sure you get her home safe and sound, or . . ."

Jonny eased herself into the passenger seat of the big sedan.

"She'll be fine, Raymond," Rasmus said. "You doin' okay?"

"I'm doin' just fine, Rasmus. Well as can be expected, I guess. You drive carefully now. That's precious cargo you carryin' there."

During the ride into town, Rasmus told Jonny to not be concerned in the event things got out of hand during the meeting. "I've been out of politics for a while now, Jonny," he said, "but I still know how it works, particularly when it doesn't work."

"What's the meeting about?" Jonny asked.

"I'd rather leave that for the mayor to outline for you," he said. "I don't want to, let's say, color anything for you in advance. I'll be participating, briefly, I'm sure, but there's a racial component to what's going to be discussed, even though some of the folks might not be able or willing to see it."

"Well," she said, "thanks for inviting me, Senator, er, Mr. Belvoir."

"We'll see after all's said and done if you will still want to thank me," he said, laughing. "You will no doubt bear witness to how just plain stupid the people the voters put into office can be when they are asked to actually do something. And I'm serious about that part, Jonquil."

When they arrived, a crowd of folks was milling around the entrance to Vosalia Town Hall, waiting for the doors to open. Closed doors apparently didn't deter the former senator from Pitts County. He ushered Jonquil around to a side entrance. A black security guard saw Rasmus approach. He smiled and let him and Jonquil in and escorted them directly to the meeting venue.

The room was empty, save for two people at the outer doors, waiting for them to open. Rasmus took a meeting agenda from one of them and handed it to Jonny. "Take a seat along the center aisle in the front row," he said. "Let the others walk around you if they want to. It's like church; no one wants to sit in the front row. Now, I don't rightly know if anyone from the media will attend, but they might. They like it when fireworks are on the agenda."

Jonny looked at him. "Fireworks?"

"The town council, as a body, hates confrontation.

Whenever it faces a dispute over land use, speed limits, parking spaces, sign ordinances, whatever, the members hem and haw and avoid tough decisions as long as humanly possible. They also hate the Vosalia open records laws they themselves put into place, the state's open meetings and public records laws, and other such barriers to simply locking the door, opening a bottle of Jim or Jack, and just working' things out.

"Tonight, the council is going to vote on the request by several of the town's leading black citizens to either take down or relocate Johnny Reb, currently residing in the park downtown. The statue serves, for those sympathetic to the South's position during the Civil War, as a fond reminder of what they view as better days gone by. To the town's black community and those others who are sympathetic to their past tribulations, the soldier represents a wink and a nod to Mississippi's embarrassing but unconditional support of slavery. They think that Confederate statue has no place in the public square.

"It's an emotional question if Johnny Reb stays or goes, and things'll get crowded and noisy in here pretty quickly. Don't worry, Jonny, just verbal fireworks. You're safe here with me."

Jonny looked over the meeting agenda. Georgia Lee Townsend, chair of the Pitts County Historical Preservation Board, would speak, representing preservation interests. Delia Scott, president of the Daughters of the Confederacy would comment on the record for what Rasmus said was referred to as "southern pride, values, and traditions." The former senator himself would make the case for Vosalia's black community and for others supportive of erasing the stain of slavery and removal or relocation of the statue. Finally, Joe Malone, CEO of the 55-22 Companies, developer of multifamily residential and retail properties between Memphis, Jackson, and Oxford, would address the council in support of progress and economic develop-ment of the park land, in the form of condominiums, apartments, stores, and offices.

Council member Allan Townsend would not be voting, since he was married to Georgia Lee Townsend of the Historic Preservation Board, and therefore had a clear conflict of interest in the proceedings. This left four votes in play, which made a 2-2 tie a distinct possibility. According to Erasmus, if this happened, it would constitute defeat of whichever of the two motions before the council happened to be in play.

Jonny looked around the room. She was buoyed by the fact that many of the seats in the council chamber were occupied by people who looked like her.

At 6:03pm, Mayor Timothy Edwards gaveled the meeting to order. He read from prepared notes.

"Good evening, y'all. We have two questions before the council this evening. The first involves whether the statue currently standing in Harold Christianson Park should be removed and relocated to the Confederate graveyard on Highway 51 north of town, with permission of the Pitts County Commission; should simply be torn down; or should be left where it is, as it is. Depending on the resolution of that question, we will take up the petition by the 55-22 Companies to purchase the park property at a price consistent with fair market real estate values in the downtown Vosalia business district and develop said property in a manner acceptable to both Vosalia and Pitts County planning and zoning officials.

"If, after hearing final arguments from Senator Belvoir, Mrs. Townsend, Mrs. Scott and Mr. Malone, the council votes against removal and relocation of Johnny Reb, the second question becomes moot and will not be taken up by the council. Each of those speaking, including and especially Mr. Belvoir, will have two minutes to sum up your case before the council. Two minutes." He held up two fingers, as if offering a peace sign. "After everyone has spoken, we will entertain up to ten one-minute comments from the public, to which the council will not, repeat, will not, respond." The mayor looked at each of the council members after making this pronouncement. They all nodded their affirmation of the mayor's charge

"Names were drawn before the meeting designating which ten residents of Vosalia will be invited to provide public comment on the primary issue before the council. Additionally, the speaking order was determined by numbered and folded pieces of paper, which were selected by our city clerk, Mrs. Phillipa Consens. Mr. Belvoir, you get to go first."

Things fell apart more quickly than all but a few of those in attendance could have predicted. Rasmus had prepared Jonny for this, as he put it, inevitability. To the surprise of absolutely no one, Erasmus Belvoir took his entire allotted two minutes, plus at least another minute and a half, petitioning the council to waive the two-minute rule because there was no possibility of him being able to address such an emotionally charged issue regarding the removal or relocation of a statue in a public space so offensive to so many residents of Vosalia, Mississippi, in only two minutes. This led to vociferous objection on the part of both Mrs. Townsend and Mrs. Scott, which in turn caused the overflow crowd in the gallery of the town council chamber to ignore calls to order and the repeated banging of the mayor's gavel, instead choosing up sides in condemnation of all points of view other than their own.

After approximately seven minutes of loud, impolite, contentious chaos and anarchy, over which he had absolutely no control, Mayor Edwards declared this meeting of the Vosalia Town Council adjourned. The entire five-member council rose as one and exited the town council chamber, leaving two security officers, in place for the sole purpose of maintaining order, to gradually move everyone outside onto South Street.

There, the assembled multitudes continued bickering. Everyone ignored the points of view presented by others unless they matched their own.

Jonny noticed Martha Plemmons, standing with her walker, outside Town Hall. She smiled when she saw Jonny approaching. "Well, Jonquil, did you learn anything in there?"

"Can't say that I did, Miss Martha," Jonny said. "Everything happened just the way Mr. Belvoir said it would. I'm not sure how I feel about that statue."

"I understand, Jonquil," Martha said. "It's not the statue itself. It's what the statue represents. It has no business, in my humble opinion, occupying space in a public park in the middle of town, but I don't know how many of the good people of Vosalia understand such subtlety."

"What do you mean?" Jonny asked.

Martha considered the question. "As I said, it's complicated, Jonquil. The statue, in a manner of speaking, celebrates the confederate South. The South wanted to keep slavery in place, and although some people"—she nodded in the direction of Delia Scott and Georgia Lee Townsend, who were engaged in some very animated discussion— "would have you believe it's just about history, it's really a history the modern south needs to acknowledge and from which it should distance itself all these years later."

Jonny and Martha watched as those two, and many of the rest of the people who were previously engaged on one side or another of the statue issue continued their spirited conversations in the cool autumn evening.

"I guess I never gave it much thought," Jonny said.

Martha smiled at her. "You're still very young, darling."

After a few moments, Rasmus made his way over to them.

"Well, Senator," Martha said, "I'd say our elected representatives here in Vosalia managed the situation about as could be expected. Would you agree?"

He threw up his hands in frustration but nodded his head. He smiled at Jonny but addressed Martha. "It's a metaphor, I believe, Martha."

"Well, that's a word I don't typically expect to hear from the lips of an attorney," she said. "A metaphor of what?"

Jonny was enjoying the tone of the conversation between the two. Belvoir stood at least a head taller than Martha Plemmons. He looked down at her as if he were about to lecture a small child.

"I watched this movie, a long time ago," he said. "All I remember about it was Ben Gazarra played the main character. Do you remember him?"

Martha smiled and nodded her head. "I do," she said. "A fine actor, as I recall, for a New Yorker."

"I wish I remembered the name of the movie. I need to use that Google or something. Anyway, he had a line in the movie I never forgot. He said, 'In real life there are questions to which there are no answers, and there are problems to which there are no solutions.'"

Jonny nodded in appreciation of the wisdom in the statement.

Martha thought for a moment. *"Saint Jack,"* she said.

"I'm sorry?"

"The name of the film, Rasmus," she said. "I believe it was called *Saint Jack.*"

He looked at her and smiled. "You know, I think you may be right."

"So, is that your metaphor?"

He shook his head. "No, Martha. This ridiculousness"—he waved his hands at the gaggle still debating the merits of what didn't get resolved at the meeting—"is a metaphor for the problems associated with race in Vosalia, in Mississippi, in America, hell, in the whole damn world. They are going to be with us for a long, long time."

"Mr. Belvoir . . ." Jonny said.

"I know. I need to get young Ms. Carter here home before her cranky old grandfather comes after me with a shotgun."

Martha smiled at Jonny. "Enjoy the ride home, Jonquil. I hope to see you again, soon. And please send my best to Raymond."

"Me too, Miss Martha," Jonny said. "And I will . . . send your best to my Poppop."

"Retired Senator Belvoir, following your foray out to the hinterlands with this charming young lady, why don't you come by and share a glass of sweet tea?" Martha asked.

He nodded. "Indeed, I will," he said. "Yes, I'll see you in a little bit."

Chapter 8

Fred Holmes paced back and forth in his upstairs bedroom. While they waited for Bobby Glass to arrive, Tommy Boggs studied the scrupulously protected shrine to the Confederacy's most impressive Civil War victory, that Fred kept on his bureau. The twenty-four by thirty-six-inch diorama featured dozens of meticulously hand painted, two-inch high, steel Confederate soldiers brandishing long guns. They were standing upright, while an even larger number of blue-clad Union soldiers were on their backs in a green field.

"What's this all about, again?" Tommy said.

Fred came over to the bureau. "In the spring of 1863, near Chancellorsville, Virginia, Lee's army put a beating on an invading Union army almost twice its size and sent them back across the Rappahannock River. Lee lost his must trusted general, though, old Stonewall Jackson. This was a gift from my grandfather, Richard Holmes."

Fred went back to pacing.

"Fred, why you wound up so damn tight about what some girl's gonna write for some stupid history paper?" Tommy asked.

Fred couldn't sit still. He paced back and forth, all the while punching his left palm with the clenched fist of his right hand. "I can't rightly say," he said. "Just pisses me off she got to bring up some old shit that's none of her damn business."

"What 'old shit'?"

"I overheard Todd Hampton's father telling him about it," Fred said. "He's the teacher. Said it was something about something that happened back in 1960."

"1960? Why are you worried about something happened fifty-some years ago? 1960? Jesus, Fred!"

Fred sat down, finally, and stared at Tommy. "You don't know about the newspaper fire, do you?" he asked.

"What newspaper fire?"

Fred shook his head. "Tommy Boggs, you are about the dumbest white person I have ever met."

Tommy stood up. "You got your nerve calling me dumb, you jackass," he said. "I'm not the one walking a hole in my bedroom rug. Now, what goddamn newspaper fire? I only moved here seven years ago from Hattiesburg."

"Yeah, that's right," Fred said. "Why would you know about that? I can't really talk about it, but I can sure tell you that no one in my family wants anyone talking about that fire."

Bobby Glass walked into the room. "What fire?" he asked. "When did that happen?"

Fred stared at the huge Stars and Bars tacked to the ceiling of his room. "I just want to . . . I need to make sure that Carter bitch don't open no can of worms involving my family."

"We still talkin' about that?" Bobby asked. "She don't mean nothing to no one, Fred." The phone rang but Fred ignored it.

"Why does any of you give a shit about some nigger girl, anyway?" he said. "You tellin' me I should just let her go ahead and smear my family's name?"

"What are you *talking* about?" Tommy asked.

There was a loud knock at the door to Fred's room. No one was permitted in his room when he and his friends were there. "Fred?" his mother, Winifred, called. "You have a phone call."

"Who is it?" he shouted.

"Don't you raise your voice at me, Fred Holmes," she said. "It's Todd Hampton."

Fred shook his head. "What does he want? Ah, never mind, I got it," he said, and picked up the extension.

"Yeah?"

"That's how you answer the phone? It's Todd Hampton, Fred."

"Yeah, my mother said. What do you want?"

"What I want is for you to stop being such an asshole."

"Who you callin'—"

"Shut up and listen. My father told me you might have overheard something about someone writing a history paper about the fire at the *Clarion*."

"Yeah, I did. That little coon bitch, Carter," Fred said. "What about it?"

"I'm just letting you know not to do anything stupid. It's a freshman history paper. It doesn't involve you."

Fred exploded. "What do you mean it don't involve me? It involves my family, my grandfather, and I'm not gonna let some little coon—"

"That's what I mean, Fred. You need to get with the program. War's over. South lost. She'll write what she wants to write and if you do anything stupid—"

"What, you'll tell your daddy?" There was a moment of silence on the line. "You still there, Hampton? What you gonna do about it?"

"I said my piece, Fred. Grow the hell up!" Todd Hampton said, and hung up.

"What do you mean, grow the hell up? Hello? You there, Hampton?"

Tommy Boggs and Bobby Glass watched as Fred slammed the phone down and started punching his palm.

"Fuck Todd Hampton. Thinks he's hot shit. I'll

show him who's hot shit. What are you two looking at? Go on. Get out. Get the fuck out!"

"Come on, Fred," Bobby said. "Why don't you just let it go? Nobody cares about it. It don't mean anything."

Fred threw the door to his room open expecting to see his mother there. Instead, she'd gone back downstairs.

"Everything all right up there, Fred? Fred?" Tommy and Bobby walked down the stairs. Fred slammed the door to his room.

❧

Saturday, October 28

Jonny opened her iPad and started assembling her notes and thoughts about the paper she wanted to write. It was due in a week, and she was uncertain as to how she was going to proceed.

"Crazy tree," she said to herself. "Why'd you have to—what am I doing? A tree? Talking to me? In a dream? Sounds like twelve different kinds of stupid, now I'm thinking about it." She began typing on the Bluetooth keyboard paired with her iPad. It had to be something that happened, not something that didn't happen. That was dumb. How could something be history if it didn't happen? Now, the newspaper fire? That actually did happen.

Jonny closed her iPad, threw it into her backpack, and stomped down the stairs and out the front door. Her grandfather was already on the porch.

"I'm going into town," she said. "I need to talk to Mr. Dellinger at the newspaper."

He nodded and stood up. "So, this mean you're writing your history paper on the *Clarion* fire?"

She moved in to hug him. "Yes, Poppop. Something that didn't happen can't be history, right? The fire happened, on May 26, 1960."

He nodded again and put his hands on her shoulders. "You're getting tall, girl."

She smiled.

"I guess I am," she said, leaning in to kiss him on the cheek. "I'll see you later."

"Before you go, you might want to call ahead. You know, make sure he's there."

"Why? Doesn't—oh, right. It's Saturday. Thanks, Poppop!" She sat on the top step, opened her iPad, and Googled "Vosalia, Mississippi *Clarion*." She closed the iPad, pulled out her phone, and punched in the number. Two minutes later she was kissing Raymond goodbye again.

"He's there! I'll see you later, Poppop." She grabbed her bike and pedaled up the long gravel driveway to the Pitts Taylor Pike.

Raymond watched Jonny until she turned onto the Pike and out of his view. "That's right. Focus on the fire, Jonny," he whispered. "Just the fire." He went inside to rustle himself up something to eat so he could take his first insulin shot of the day.

Jonny and Jeff Dellinger sat on opposite sides of his desk in his small, glass enclosed corner office alongside the *Clarion*'s small newsroom. His office was awash in paper, books, magazines, and journals. A flat panel TV on top of a file cabinet played CNN with the volume turned down and closed captioning running six seconds behind the moving lips of the talking heads.

"How do you work in all this clutter?" Jonny asked.

He laughed. "Newspaper people are notoriously messy, Jonquil," he said.

"My Poppop would call this a firetrap," she said, and immediately regretted her unfiltered comment. "I'm sorry, Mr. Dellinger," she said. "I know we're going to be looking for information about the fire back in 1960. I didn't mean . . ." He smiled at her.

"Your grandfather would be absolutely correct," he said. "I should clean up, but I'm afraid what I might find buried in all this mess. Come around here. I have something to show you."

Jonny pulled her chair around the desk, carefully avoiding a trashcan filled with what looked to her like unopened mail. The screen on his MacBook revealed a small story in a column headlined, "Around the Region," in the *Memphis Press-Scimitar*. It was dated May 29, 1960. Jonny read:

NW Mississippi Weekly Newspaper
Destroyed by Fire

A fire last Thursday gutted the offices of the *Pitts County Clarion*, a weekly newspaper in Vosalia, Mississippi. No one was injured, but the Pitts County Fire Department is investigating the possibility the fire was intentionally started.

"We received an anonymous tip implicating two local men," said Wendell Kohl, Pitts County's fire chief. "We expect the sheriff to interview these individuals first thing in the morning."

A spokesman for the Pitts County Sheriff's Department could not confirm whether the fire at the *Clarion* had anything to do with reports of gunshots heard along the Pitts Taylor Pike following the fire.

"There's a similar brief in the Oxford daily newspaper, the *Eagle*," Jeff said. "We couldn't publish for almost a month after this happened, but one of our people back then must have put something out on one of the wire services."

"What's a wire service?" Jonny asked, but another

more interesting question for her hung, for the moment, unasked.

"Wire services provide subscriber newspapers with stories from outside their ADI; that's area of dominant influence," he said. "Associated Press, United Press International, Copley News Service . . . these are wire services we subscribed to back then to get filler content for our newspaper."

She had several questions about these services. Instead, she cocked her head and simply said, "We? Our?"

He smiled. "Oh, of course. Why would you know? The *Clarion* has been owned by the Dellinger family since back before the Great Depression," he said. "My great-grandfather, grandfather, and father all served as editor, publisher, reporter, and advertising salesman. In big city newspapers, like the *Press-Scimitar* in Memphis used to be, different people do all those jobs. In small towns, there are typically only a handful of people on staff."

Jonny looked at him. "So, you own the *Clarion* now?"

"I do, Jonny," he said. "After my accident I hired two people to perform those tasks, but I'm still owner and publisher and plan to be here for the foreseeable future."

Jonny nodded her understanding. "Okay, so after the fire someone called these wire services and told them what happened? Are any of those people still around?"

"One is, for sure," he said. "If I remember our first conversation, your grandfather hasn't been much help about all this. Have I got that right?" Jonny nodded.

"He's actually been no help at all," she said. "Everyone's been trying to get me to write about something else. Him, my teacher Mr. Hampton, Miss Plemmons . . ."

Jeff sat up straight. "You talked to Martha Plemmons?"

"Yes, I have. I met her in the library, and Miss Faraday, you know her, she told me to talk to Miss Plemmons."

"Hmmm," he said. "Didn't she tell you . . ." He stopped.

"Tell me what? You know . . . Wait. Did she work here back then?"

Jeff Dellinger started drumming his fingers on the desk, avoiding Jonny's eyes, and pursing his lips.

"She did, didn't she?" Jonny asked.

"Look, Jonny," he said, "there are things associated with the fire and with how things were back then that you really need to learn from the people involved who are still alive. It would be wrong for me to—" Jonny stood up. She looked at him and smiled.

"I know a lot more now than I did when I came to see you this morning, Mr. Dellinger," she said. "You've been more helpful than you probably know."

CHAPTER 9

"Come on in, Jonquil," Martha called in response to the urgent knock.

Jonny walked in and put her backpack on the upholstered chair just inside the front door.

"I'm sorry to bother you again, Miss Plemmons."

Martha was in her living room, holding a book. "First of all, you're not bothering me, Jonquil. Second, we agreed you'd call me Martha, and third, I'm sorry I didn't tell you I worked at the *Clarion* back then, but you didn't ask."

Jonny smiled. "He called you."

Now, Martha smiled. "Yes, he did."

"Were you there—"

Martha put her hand up. "Would you care for some sweet tea, dear?"

Jonny followed Martha into the kitchen. Martha took two glasses out of a cabinet over her sink. She looked at both, to make sure they were clean.

"Jonquil, would you please get the pitcher of tea from the refrigerator?"

Jonny did as she was asked, brought the pitcher to the counter, and poured sweet tea into both glasses.

"Which glass would you prefer?" Martha asked. The glasses were the same.

Jonny selected one of the glasses with her right hand and picked up the other glass with her left. Martha pushed her walker into the living room, with Jonny following.

"Please," Martha Plemmons said, "have a seat anywhere, Jonquil."

Jonny sat so she could face the old woman. She took a sip of her tea.

"Miss—Martha, were you at the newspaper the day of the fire?"

Martha thought for a moment and nodded. "If I recall correctly, it was a Thursday," she said. "The town was getting ready for Decoration Day; that's what we used to call Memorial Day. There'd be a parade, some speeches at the gazebo that used to be across from the old Town Hall on South Street." She hesitated, as if trying to collect memories from long ago.

"I worked at the *Clarion*. I must have been twenty-one, twenty-two-years old. I answered the telephone and sold classified advertisements. It was a good job. I enjoyed it. I'd just returned from attending the Mississippi State College for Women. It was just for white women back then. Now, the school has black students, and even some men. Trust me, Jonny, given enough time, almost everything changes."

"But not every*one* changes, right, Martha?"

"Indeed! That's true. I'm sorry, Jonquil . . . I studied English in college. What I just did is called a digression."

Jonny smiled but remained silent. Martha looked at point on the wall behind Jonquil somewhere above her head.

"Yes, Jonquil, I was there, in the office. A nice young man helped me move a large file cabinet from the middle of the front room into an alcove between two offices. The offices belonged to Mr. Dellinger, who owned and published the newspaper, and his son, Clark. Clark was the current Mr. Dellinger's father. They're both gone now.

"I don't recall the exact time; it wasn't dark, but it was early evening, I believe. We heard windows breaking, and then the fire started. We escaped through the side door, onto Stuart Street. I couldn't understand for the life of me why anyone would want to burn down the newspaper."

Jonny had more questions. Who was "we?" Did Martha know the two men who were arrested, Collins and Holmes? Did she ever learn why they wanted to burn down the newspaper?

"Once again, Jonquil, those were very difficult times in the south. After the Supreme Court did away with that whole 'separate but equal' nonsense tensions rose between white people and black people throughout the region, including here. Angry people sometimes did things for no reason other than they were angry people. I didn't know either of those two men." Martha took a drink of tea. "If it's okay with you, Jonquil, I'd like to rest for a while. Perhaps we can talk about this again, maybe one day next week after you finish at school."

Jonny walked over, bent down and gave the old woman a hug. "You're so nice to talk to me, Miss—Martha," she said. "Is there anything I can help with before you rest?"

Martha smiled. "You can take those glasses into the kitchen and put them in the sink, if you please, Jonquil. Please send my very best regards to your grandfather, would you?"

Jonny turned toward the door but stopped. "You told me last time you knew my grandmother and my parents."

"I did," Martha said. "Not well, of course, but I did. Perhaps we can talk about that next time as well, okay?"

Jonny nodded. "Sure. You get you some rest, Martha.

Monday, October 30

Jonny's paper for Mr. Hampton's history class needed to be more than five hundred words but fewer than one thousand words. So far, she had collected a handful of facts about what happened in the early evening hours of May 26, 1960 at the corner of South and Stuart Streets in Vosalia. She knew of no one she could talk to about why Richard Holmes and Arthur Collins had started the fire.

She'd learned in an earlier language arts class that a good paper needed to address questions of who, what, when, where, how, and why. She knew everything except why. If she could find out *why*, Jonny was pretty sure she'd have herself an "A" paper.

After history class, Jonny joined the rest of the girls' track team behind the school on the 400-meter oval. Several of her teammates had completed their practice for the day, long jumping, pole-vaulting, running heats in the 100- and 200-meter sprints and hurdles, and the 400-meter hurdles. The cross-country runners were covering a ten-mile road course winding through town, and out of town along the Pitts Taylor Pike, and back. When Jonny arrived, she nodded at her coach and quickly stripped down to her shorts, leggings, and track team tank over a long-sleeved T-shirt. She put on her shoes, stretched, and jogged around the oval twice to warm up. She'd run five or six 400-meter sprints, in different lanes on the track, hoping to match or beat her personal best time of just under fifty-nine seconds. By the time she'd completed her regimen and cooled down she was alone on the track. She checked her watch. It was a few minutes past 6:00 pm.

Jonny sat cross-legged on the track and logged her times in her personal journal. Sanya Richards of St. Thomas Aquinas High School in Fort Lauderdale, Florida held the high school world record of 50.69 seconds in the 400 meters. Jonny had a long way to go before she'd even come close to approaching that time, but she was only fourteen. Sanya set that record when she was eighteen and was a full-grown young woman with years of track competition behind her.

As Jonny jogged into the school parking lot, Tommy Boggs, Fred Holmes, and Bobby Glass jumped out of a truck and spread themselves so Jonny would either have to stop or try to go around them. As soon as she stopped, Fred Holmes moved forward and put his face inches away from hers.

"What do you want?" she said. Once again, she had no intention of cowering in front of a bully.

"I want you to die, bitch," he said. His two friends moved closer.

"No plan to do that any time soon," she said. "Now please get out my face, and tell your two boys to do the same, okay?"

Fred pushed Jonny, managing to get one of his hands onto one of her breasts in the process. Bobby laughed.

"How'd that feel, Fred?" Bobby asked. "She got her some nice little titties there?"

Bobby moved closer to Jonny. He reached out and touched her left breast. She slapped his hand away. She thought briefly about using some of the self-defense training she'd learned at school, but so far, the boys had done little but talk.

"I don't think there's nothin' there at all," Bobby said. "Maybe she's really a he."

The three of them kept moving forward, slowly, finally causing Jonquil, who was backtracking, to trip over the inner-lane guard to the running track. Fred stepped in and reached down a hand. "You need some help, nigger?" he asked. Jonny executed a backward roll and jumped to her feet.

"You need three of you to push around one fourteen-year-old girl?" she asked. "I don't know what you jerks have in mind, but I guarantee at least one of you is gonna get—"

Fred moved in and took a swing with his right fist. She moved. He missed. The punch glanced off her shoulder but hurt enough for her to reach up to massage her upper arm. Tommy stepped in. This time she didn't wait. She kicked him hard, right in the crotch. If he'd been a football, he'd have flown thirty yards. He went down like a sack of seed.

"You bitch," he said. "I was just gonna mess you up a little but now . . ."

Bobby Glass moved behind Jonquil and grabbed her around her arms and chest. She threw her head back hard, and the sound she heard meant she had possibly broken his nose. Fred moved in quickly and started punching, first her arms, then her face and body. He backed up to admire his handiwork. She stepped forward and kicked him between his legs.

"Motherfucker," he croaked, joining his friend on his knees.

Jonny caught a glimpse of someone running across the track. He'd apparently seen enough. He punched Fred Holmes hard, in the back of his head, knocking him onto the dirt track. He turned to face Bobby Glass, who was trying to stop the bleeding from his nose.

"Get the hell out of here, all of you." Jonquil recognized Todd Hampton's voice.

Fred turned around and stepped back. "I can't believe this," he said. "You're taking her side?"

"I can't believe it took three of you jackasses to almost get over on one fourteen-year-old freshman girl," he said. "I can't wait to let the rest of the school know how she got two of you on the ground and bloodied the third one's nose. Bunch of damn losers."

Jonquil was on her knees with her head down. She'd taken a beating.

"You three leave now and maybe the only thing gets hurt is your ignorant racist pride," Todd said. "Get outta here! Now!" he shouted.

They limped back to Fred's truck. "This ain't over, Hampton," Fred said. "Just 'cause your father's a teacher . . ."

"This damn well better be over, Fred. I told you when I talked to you the other day. You three need to get your shit together, or I may let her have another go at you. One-on-one, one at a time, next time." They got into Fred's truck. He kicked up a bunch of gravel leaving the parking lot.

Jonquil smiled at Pitts County High School's quarterback and golden boy. He kept his dark brown hair long but not too long. He had dark brown eyes and a diamond-shaped face, with strong cheekbones.

"I probably could handle them one at a time," Jonny said. "Thanks a lot, Todd."

"They're idiots," he said. "I'm just glad you're okay."

He looked at her. She had a bruise on her eye and a split, swollen lip.

"You know, I really can't believe this," she said. "I know how stuff is. This isn't the first time I've had to put up with racist crap, but nobody ever got physical with me before." She looked at him. "When is this shit going to end?"

"I don't know," he said. "I'm going to keep an eye on those three for a while. You let me know if they hassle you anymore, okay?"

She smiled at him. "Yeah, I will. But I got a couple of 'em pretty good, right?"

He smiled back at her. "You got all of them pretty good, and it was a sight to see."

Todd Hampton walked her over near where he'd parked his own truck. "Let me give you a ride home. Or, at least out to the pike?"

"I can't imagine what your father's going to say when he sees me tomorrow."

"Don't worry about that," Todd said. "I'll give him a heads up when I see him. Come on, let me drive you home."

There wasn't much talking during the ten-minute drive from Pitts County High School to the long, straight driveway leading from their mailbox to the Steadman house. Todd kept looking at her, but Jonny kept her own eyes straight ahead. When they arrived, he retrieved Jonny's bike from the bed of his truck.

"You gonna be alright?"

"I'm okay," she said. "My grandfather's gonna throw a fit, though." She looked at him. "Thanks again, Todd. I really appreciate what you did today."

"Just take care of yourself," he said. "We need you at regionals and then at state next spring."

She smiled back. "Hey, Todd?" He turned his head. "Just so you know, I'll be fifteen in about a month." It was his turn to smile at her as he drove away.

Jonny locked her bike on the fence post along the north side of the driveway. She gingerly put her arm through the strap of her backpack and jogged up to the house. She noticed the porch was empty, but lights were on inside, and Raymond's truck was under the carport where he always parked it.

Old man's probably cooking dinner. She opened the screen door.

Raymond wasn't cooking dinner. The old man was lying unconscious on the rug in the front room.

Chapter 10

They'd talked about this at least once a year since Raymond felt Jonny was old enough to understand what was happening, and then to act. She looked at her grandfather and immediately grabbed the house phone.

"911," the woman's voice said after one ring. "What's the nature of your emergency?"

"I think his blood sugar crashed," Jonny said. "Raymond Steadman, age seventy-eight, er, seventy-nine, I'm not sure." She recited her address.

"Can you make sure he has a pulse?"

Jonny picked up her grandfather's right hand. It was warm. She felt the inside of his wrist using her first and second fingers. She found his pulse, closed her eyes, and counted.

"Yes," she said. "Approximately fifty-four, fifty-five."

"Hmmm. That's shallow. EMT is on the way. Do you have anything …?"

"Yes," Jonny said. "Hold on." She ran into the kitchen, opened the pantry, and grabbed a packet of grape Kool-Aid Raymond kept in the house for exactly this sort of emergency. She ripped it open, opened his mouth and poured it onto his tongue. She got a glass of water and poured a small amount into his mouth. About ten seconds later, he began to come around.

"He's waking up," she said to the operator.

"Good," she said. "And good work. EMT should be there right about now."

Jonny saw the ambulance come to a screeching stop a few feet from the steps to the front porch. The EMTs jumped out, opened the back door to the ambulance, grabbed a gurney, and entered the house. Raymond was halfway sitting up, groggy, holding a red Solo cup of water.

"How you doin' young fella?" the first EMT asked. His badge indicated his name was Robert Caldecott.

The second EMT placed a blood pressure cuff on Raymond's left arm and began squeezing the ball. "Looks high . . . 156 over 110," he said. "How're you feeling, sir?" His badge identified him as Shaun Monroe. "This young lady over here likely saved your life today, you know that?"

Raymond looked at Jonny and smiled, weakly. "Yeah," he said. "Probably saved my life the day she was born."

"I think the worst is over here," Caldecott said, "but

we're going to check you in to Vo-Med for observation and a whole bunch of poking and prodding. You up for that?"

"I don't know," Raymond said. "Who's going to look after . . ." He nodded off again. They lifted him onto the rolling gurney and walked him out the front door.

"Can I ride with you?" Jonny asked.

"I don't know," Monroe said. "You like Marshall Tucker Band?"

She smiled. "I don't know who that is," she said.

He smiled and gave a flick of his head toward his partner. "I'll see if we can find something better. Come on."

❧

Wanda, the nurse who admitted Raymond at Vosalia Medical Center told him that Jonny did everything right. Fully awake by this time, Raymond was more interested in why Jonny had a fat lip and contusions on her face and upper left arm.

"Ah," Jonny said, "I took a flop on the track, Poppop. Nothin' that ain't happened before." This wasn't the time for her to reveal what really went on.

Wanda settled Raymond into the bed he'd sleep in that night and then signaled Jonny to walk outside with her.

"I'd like to clean that lip, the cut under your eye, and the scrapes on your arm," she said. "And while I do that, you can tell me what really happened."

Jonny nodded at her. "It's no big thing," she said. "Just some dumb-ass rednecks. Pretty sure they're hurting worse than I am." Wanda smiled and high-fived with Jonny.

"Will I be able to stay with him tonight?" she asked.

"I don't see why not," Wanda said. "Can you sleep in a chair, or should I find you a cot somewhere?" Jonny told her the chair would be fine.

After Wanda cleaned up her minor wounds, Jonny returned to Raymond's room. He was awake but staring at the blinds over the window.

"You are studying on something pretty hard over there, old man," she said.

He looked at her, smiled, and pointed at the Styrofoam cup filled with ice chips. "I'm drier than the bark on that nasty old talking tree of yours, Jonquil," he whispered.

She smiled and let him take whatever he wanted from the cup. "Tree's been quiet these past few days," she said.

He snorted. "I guess you need to be, what you called it, doing *research* so you can hear it, right? Research, my left elbow," he said. "I call it snoozin'."

"I'll see if it's got anything new to say tomorrow, Poppop."

"I need you to call someone for me," he said. "Maybe two or three someone's."

"Why? You ain't goin' nowhere."

He looked at her, softly, lovingly. "You it, Jonquil," he said. "You all I got; you know?"

She put her hands on the sides of his forehead and kissed him above the bridge of his nose. "Same here, you old coot. Who you want me to call?"

She made the phone calls he'd requested. After the calls, she told him about her second meeting with Martha Plemmons. "Did you know she was in the office when those jackasses set fire to the newspaper?"

He smiled. "She told you that?"

"How else would I know?"

"She tell you anything else about that day?"

"Not too much," Jonny said. "Were you living out where we are now when that happened?"

"In the neighborhood," he said, "but not right in the same house we at now."

She told him about the two stories from the Memphis and Oxford newspapers, about people reporting shots being fired out on the pike. "Mr. Dellinger told me . . . did you know he owns the newspaper?"

Raymond laughed and nodded. "Yep, I did. Him, his daddy, and his daddy's daddy before him. That newspaper is the Dellinger family's business."

Jonny was thoughtful for a moment. "Someone must have had it in for the Dellinger family, right? Why else would they try to burn the newspaper down?"

Elijah Hampton walked into the room, followed by his son, Jesse, and Jesse's son, Todd. Jonny smiled at her teacher and at her knight in shining armor. Jesse signaled her to slip outside the room.

"Does he know what happened to you?" he asked her.

She shook her head. "Not yet. I'll tell him when he's better," she said. "Your son . . . he maybe saved my life today."

Her teacher chuckled. "Not to hear him tell it, Jonquil. He told me those legs of yours helped level the playing field."

"Yeah," she said, sheepishly, "but there were three of them. I'm real glad he's not like them."

"None of us are like them," he said. "Thanks for calling my father, by the way. How's your granddad doing?"

She told him what she did when she got home and what they knew at the hospital. "They're keeping him at least overnight for tests and rest. I'm gonna stay here with him." Jesse told her not to worry about school the next day; he'd collect her assignments and have Todd bring them either to the hospital or the house.

When they walked back to Raymond's room, Erasmus Belvoir was holding court.

"You see? You see? Those damned Oreo cookies gonna be the end for you, Turtle," he said. "Why you eat those damn things anyway? Don't you know the word Oreo is a slur black people use on other black people?"

Jonny looked skeptically at the former state senator.

"Oh, you probably don't know about this, young lady," he said. "Sometimes, some of the more, how do I say this, vociferous, impatient members of the black community try to insult black elected officials when we can't or won't immediately just snap our fingers to change everything they want us to. They call us Oreos."

"I'm sorry, Senator—Mr. Belvoir. I just don't know what that means."

"First of all, it's nice to see you again, Jonquil. Now what I mean is, an Oreo, besides being a weapon of destruction for people like your grandfather, is . . ." He looked at Raymond, who nodded. "An Oreo is dark on the outside and white on the inside. There you have it." They all had a good laugh.

Raymond nodded. "Only had six of 'em," he mumbled.

"*Six of them?*" Jonny shrieked. "Six? You are one crazy old man, Poppop. You ate six Oreos, all at one time?"

"Yes, I did," he said. "What you gonna do about it?"

The door to the room opened, and Martha Plemmons pushed her walker inside. She took in the scene. "Well, if this isn't perhaps the most eclectic collection of Pitts County citizens I have ever seen assembled in one room," she said. "Turtle, is it you who caused all this ruckus?"

Raymond smiled. "Hello, Martha," he said. "God, it feels like forever since I've seen you."

For a moment, the room went silent. They took

one another in. Rasmus Belvoir and the younger two of the three generations of Hampton men seized the opportunity to wish Raymond well, to tell Jonny how proud they were of how she handled his blood sugar event, and to say their good-byes. Rasmus told Raymond he'd be back.

"I'll walk these folks outside," Elijah said. "Be back in a minute or two."

Jonny watched Martha and her grandfather stare at one another.

"How long has it been, Raymond?" Martha asked him. "I remember where it was, but I don't recall exactly when it was." She looked at Jonny. "I know that sounds ridiculous, Jonquil, but—"

"It was Tonya's funeral," he said. "Would have been four days after this one here was born. December 13, 2002. If I didn't say it at the time, thank you for being there."

"Funerals, Raymond," she said. "First Jacinta, then Tonya." She turned to Jonny. "I didn't get to your father's funeral, Jonquil. He was brought home from Afghanistan and buried next to your mother while I was in the hospital. It was the one here in Vosalia before this one was built. A ruptured appendix if you can imagine." She turned back to Raymond. "And you did thank me for coming to Tonya's funeral." Then, to Jonny again, "I taught your mother how to play the piano, Jonquil, when she was a little girl. She was one of my best students." Jonny nodded and smiled.

"If you two will excuse me for a few minutes, I'm gonna see if I can find something to eat," Jonny said. She went to her backpack to get her wallet but remembered she'd removed it when she was in the ambulance with her grandfather and the EMTs. She'd placed it in the pocket of her sweat suit. It held copies of his insurance information. "You want some Famous Amos, Poppop?" He couldn't help but laugh.

"Yeah, Jonny, bring me a whole, big ol' bag, okay?" He looked at Martha. "I'm in here 'cause of cookies, Martha. Git goin'," he said to his granddaughter.

Jonny found the cafeteria, grabbed a tray and before she knew it had wolfed down a plate full of grilled chicken, mashed potatoes, and glazed carrots. She spent the next half hour wondering about the nature of the relationship between her grandfather and Miss Martha Plemmons. While she was sitting in the cafeteria, she noticed Elijah Hampton passing by on his way back to her grandfather's room.

"I don't think she's put all the pieces together just yet," Raymond said. "But she's gettin' close. She tell you about the talking tree?"

"I'm sorry, Raymond," Martha said. "I thought I just heard you say the . . . the talking tree?"

"I already told Elijah about it." He took her through his version of the two episodes Jonny had in the company of the dying oak in the back yard.

"I need to understand this," she said. "She was sitting under the tree doing something on her device; she fell asleep; and the tree told her, while she was dreaming, about the date and about a lynching?"

He shrugged. "About something that didn't happen," he said. "Right then you sounded just like Elijah did when I told him about it."

Martha Plemmons joined the two men in the land of headshaking disbelief.

"Honestly, I don't know what to make of it, Martha," Raymond said. "All I know is, she got the date right, and I suppose she got the other part right."

Martha moved over to a chair next to the bed. She patted Raymond's hand. "You have any thoughts about how something like that might have happened? Besides the possibility, however remote, that the tree did, in fact, communicate that information directly to her?"

He shook his head. "You know, I did tell her the whole story about that day when she was a baby, maybe, I don't know, a year old, maybe less," he said. "There's no way she could have held onto that kind of stuff without it coming up and out of her before now. Am I right? Martha? Elijah?"

Elijah looked to the heavens and shook his head. "No idea, Turtle. None whatsoever," he said.

Martha smiled at him and squeezed his hand. "Oh, who knows, Raymond?" she said. "Life is so mysterious. Perhaps that story you told her when she was a baby got filed away somewhere in her tiny brain until something came along and triggered the memory. Otherwise, how do you think . . .?"

Raymond gestured toward Elijah. "I'm like him. I got no earthly idea," he said. "None."

"Well," she said, "I see you've managed to maintain your friendship with Elijah Hampton here."

"Oh yeah. He's a good man, a very good man," he said.

Elijah smiled. "You don't get out much anymore, Turtle, so you may not understand this. There are a whole lot more good people around here than you might imagine," he said.

Raymond took a moment to ponder his situation. He knew diabetes would get him one day unless something else got him sooner. He hated Jonny was the one who found him, but he was happy they'd talked about what she needed to do in the event something like this ever happened. Martha broke the silence with the same thought Raymond had been mulling.

Martha said, "Maybe, you know, just maybe, it's time—"

Jonny walked into the room, noticed them disengaging their hands from one another, and smiled. "Time for what? More cookies?" she said, with a broad grin.

Raymond and Martha shared a look. She nodded. He took in a deep breath and let it out slowly.

"Jonquil, you have a seat in that chair over there," Raymond said, pointing to the green, vinyl-covered chair with big armrests under the wall-mounted television. "I want to tell you a story, and I'd appreciate it if you could manage to keep yourself quiet until I'm done. Think you can do that?"

Jonquil made a zipping motion across her lips. Elijah nodded his approval.

"I should leave," Martha said.

"Nope," he said. "Oh, no, you a part of this, Martha. You and Elijah here can jump in whenever you need to correct whatever I get wrong." Jonny's expression became serious.

"It's time for you to hear, for the second time in your life, what really happened on that date you been fixed on."

"I knew it!" she said. "I knew it. I knew it. I just knew it!"

"I don't think you know what you're about to hear, Jonquil," Elijah said. "We three in this room the only ones alive who know the whole miserable story."

Chapter 11

"It was a typical late spring Thursday in Vosalia," Raymond said. "It was warm but not nearly as hot as it would be in another month or two. Still, it was humid and cloudy. Town workers were dressin' up downtown Vosalia for the upcoming parade. In four days, that would be Monday, the thirtieth, children would get out of school early and would fill the sidewalks along the parade route. They would carry US flags and plenty of Confederate flags, and they'd wave to passing cars filled with veterans from as far back, in at least two cases, if I recall correctly, as the Spanish-American War. Others, from the so-called 'Great War,' World War II, and the Korean conflict would all be there."

"In fact, though," Martha said, "as nearly everyone in Pitts County would gladly affirm, Memorial Day, or Decoration Day as we old-timers referred to it, was all about the four years between April 12, 1861, and

May 9, 1865, when our proud, beautiful nation did everything in its power to tear itself apart.

"In Vosalia, among whites, anyway, it was referred to as 'The War of Northern Aggression.' Around the south, people also called it the War of the Rebellion, the War of Secession, or the War of Southern Independence. Confederate diehards, and we had many of those here back in the day, proudly proclaimed it the Second American Revolution. Five years short of a century after its official end and following the *Brown v. Board of Education* decision and increasing talk of civil rights, the Civil War was very much alive and well on the streets of Vosalia, Mississippi."

"I wasn't there for the parade on Decoration Day," Raymond said, "but if I had to guess there were some idiots marchin' down South Street wearin' hoods and sheets."

Martha looked at him. "The Klan was there," she said. "Civil War never ended for those reprobates."

"It was also front and center," Elijah said, "in the hearts, memories, and minds of at least two other local, ignorant, white residents. Their names were Richard Holmes and Arthur Collins. These two men were among maybe two dozen employees of Vosalia and Pitts County who were at work hanging flags and signs in anticipation of the upcoming festivities. I would have been there working as well, but I had other business, family business, in town that day."

Martha said, "Every now and then, they and others

would retreat from their duties to guzzle iced Kool-Aid laced with Tennessee sipping whiskey or whatever other spirit had been donated or confiscated for the benefit of the cause. By 3:00 p.m., much to the consternation of the ladies from the Historical Preservation Board, who were tasked with overseeing the labors of the day, most of the town workers were visibly impaired."

"That means they were drunk, Jonny," Raymond said. She nodded.

"And," Martha said, "they were having way more fun than the Daughters of the Confederacy could laugh off."

"Collins and Holmes," Elijah said, "for example, were no longer permitted access to the ladders necessary for them to secure flags to light poles along the route of the parade. Instead, they and my pathetic excuse for a brother, Samuel, watched from the front seat of Sam's pickup truck. What they saw was, I guess in their eyes, disconcerting, just plain wrong, even."

"They saw me," Raymond said, "a young, strong black man, wearing the uniform of the United States Army. I had just dropped off a book at the high school library. Black people couldn't use the public library back then." Jonny desperately wanted to ask about a thousand questions but was determined to wait until the story was finished.

"I was walking up South Street," Raymond said, "heading for Folsom, where I'd planned to turn, walk to the Pitts Taylor Pike, and return home. Home back then was where my parents were finishing up a day's work sharecropping hay and soybeans for Sam Hampton. As I passed Stuart Street, a certain young woman, who I did not know at the time, asked me for some help." Martha nodded.

"What the men in the truck saw was a 'colored boy' chatting amiably with a young white woman in front of a converted house on South Street that happened to be occupied by the *Pitts County Clarion*," Martha said.

"By this time, Collins and Holmes had consumed a great deal of the spiked punch and were both well beyond just mildly intoxicated," Elijah said. "My brother Sam, however, was stone cold sober and allowed his rage at what he saw to consume him inside the cab of his truck. He told me his version of events when I spoke with him directly the next day.

"'Ain't right' was all Sam could say, over and over, while his friends and fellow members of the local chapter of the Imperial Knights of the Ku Klux Klan managed to nod in drunken agreement. It's important for you to remember, Jonquil," said Elijah, "this was almost sixty years ago." Jonny nodded her still incomplete understanding of the situation, and its place in Vosalia history.

"Martha and I walked together up the stairs into the *Clarion's* building and closed the front door behind us," Raymond said.

"I guess Sam's prejudicial ignorance and anger bubbled over, blinding him and his drunk fool friends to any possibly innocent understanding of what was happening between these two young people they'd stumbled across," Elijah said. "Instead, their imaginations were fired by every fear involving any interaction at all between a black man and a white woman. That fear had been drummed into our heads by most all our parents, as it had in the south going back a century or more before we were even officially a nation.

"'We cannot, we will not let this go on unchallenged for a single second longer,' Sam told me he said to his fellow travelers. He started his truck. The three of them left and headed for the house where Arthur Collins still lived with his mama and daddy."

"While they were doing what they were doing," Martha said, "I explained to your grandfather what my problem was. A brand-new steel file cabinet had been delivered to the office earlier in the morning. The driver of the Sears and Roebuck delivery truck managed to get the cabinet up the stairs and through the front door but claimed he was not permitted to go any further. There was just no way I could move this thing by myself into the alcove where Mr. Dellinger wanted it. Now, my job at the *Clarion* did not include moving furniture or for that matter, office supplies, beyond reams of paper and boxes of staples and paper clips. I managed to shove it out of the way of the front door but wasn't physically able to move it by myself to where it was supposed to be.

"Now, had either Mr. Dellinger or his son, Clark, the *Clarion*'s only reporter, been present, one or both of them could easily have moved the cabinet to its designated destination. Both, however, were at a meeting of the town council regarding the upcoming Decoration Day parade and other festivities, leaving me alone to handle things in their absence."

"I looked at the situation and took off my hat," Raymond said, picking up the thread. "As I remember, I had almost no hair back then. We wore our hair as short as possible in the army. Now, I was strong, in good shape, and in the prime of my life. I'd already been in service for nearly five years. In about two, two and a half weeks, I was scheduled to leave for Friedberg, the same post in the central part of West Germany where Elvis Presley had served not quite a year and a half earlier. He and I both wore the patch of the United States Army's Third Armored Division. And we were both very proud of our service. I think I can safely say that's all Elvis and me had in common. Although the boy could sing.

"I told Martha I could handle this for her. I put my hands on the cabinet and duck-walked it, gentle as I could, the dozen or so feet from the center of the front room into an alcove between the offices of the two Mr. Dellinger's. I stepped back, made sure the cabinet was where Miss Plemmons told me she wanted it. I asked her if it was okay, and she smiled and said, 'My name is Martha. Martha Plemmons. Thank you so very much.' She must have noticed the two stripes on my sleeve. 'Corporal?' she asked me.

"I told her my name and said something like, 'You are most welcome.' I reached for my hat but," Raymond looked at Martha, "I guess she wasn't ready for me to leave just yet."

"Instead, I said to him, 'may I offer you something to drink, Corporal Steadman'?" Martha said.

"You have to keep in mind, Jonny, I was the son of black sharecroppers. The three of us, along with two hired field hands, farmed eighty acres of land owned by Sam Hampton out off the pike. That's two forty-acre tracts. The farm produced hay and soybeans, but Sam was considering changing over to poultry, which"— he looked at Elijah— "I guess was potentially more profitable."

"Yes, it was," Elijah said. "Jethro Hampton, my father, who had died from lung cancer two years earlier, had been more enthusiastic about the move to chickens than Sam was. Sam preferred the traditional cash crops, which could be worked by sharecroppers, whose status Sam viewed as only slightly above that of slaves. Now, Sam and I thought differently about almost everything. I ran the numbers and told my daddy the move to chickens made sense.

"I told him it's easier work, requires fewer hands, and has more growth potential than hay and soy. I told him I believed we had a bigger future in chicken. My argument carried the day with my father but not with Sam."

"Anyway," Raymond said, "I remember saying something like, 'I don't know, Miss—Martha. You know, we shouldn't, really.'"

Martha said, "I told him, 'Oh, fiddle faddle, Raymond, the world is changing, and you're a soldier. Besides, no one can see us, and all we're doing is sharing some sweet tea.'"

"Who could argue with that?" Raymond asked. "We talked, drank sweet tea, and learned about one another. As the day turned to dusk, Martha took the opportunity to introduce me to the game of cribbage."

Jonny smiled, recalling when Raymond taught her how to play the game.

"When 8:00 p.m. rolled around, with neither James nor Clark Dellinger returning, I cleaned up my work area, washed the glasses and pitcher we'd emptied, put away the cribbage cards, pegs, and board, and turned off the inside lights. I told your grandfather I'd been very pleased to make his acquaintance."

"I was the nervous one," Raymond said. "I told her maybe sometime in the future we'll be able to talk to one another without having to . . . you know."

"I told him, I'm afraid this part of the south is still in the dark ages," Martha said. "It's likely going to be a while before we can do something like that."

They stopped talking and looked at each other. It

was becoming increasingly clear to Jonny they both knew back then there was something going on that simply could not happen. Not for those two people, not in that place, not at that time.

Elijah picked up the story. "I was in town looking for my brother, when I noticed Arthur Collins and Richard Holmes had been staring nonstop into the window of the *Clarion* offices. They were parked in Arthur's Chevrolet pickup on the side street where they could see the drama of their own and my brother's twisted imagination playing out. Arthur and Richard didn't know who Raymond was. They found out later from Sam, when he told them of the sharecropping relationship between the Hampton and Steadman families.

"They had to be wondering what Martha was doing. Why was a white girl, a pretty one, at that, even talking to a black man?"

"It was just the way of the world back then, Jonquil," Martha said. She sighed. "It was just the way the world was." Jonny nodded.

Elijah said, "I guess Collins and Holmes had sobered up somewhat, but they must have been far from clear headed. I drove slowly through the streets of Vosalia looking for my brother. I needed Samuel's signature in order to access funds for equipment associated with the transition, on my land, from soy and hay to poultry farming. I worked my way up and down South Street looking for Sam's truck. I stopped my own truck when I spotted Collins and Holmes exiting Arthur's truck with bottles in their hands." Elijah shook his head. "I saw Holmes say something to Collins. I guess he was giving Arthur instructions.

"Collins took out a Zippo lighter and lit the rag stuffed in the neck of his bottle. Holmes climbed onto the porch of the *Clarion* offices, lit the rag in his own bottle, and hurled it through the front window, seconds after Collins did the same through the first back window he came to."

"I heard the noise but had no idea what had happened," Martha said. "I asked Raymond what it was."

"I heard glass shatter," Raymond said. "We moved into the foyer, and I saw right away the front rooms were in flames. I told her we needed to get out, right now. I grabbed her hand and pulled her toward the back door."

"The back rooms were filled with stacks of old newspapers," Martha said. "They had already started to fill with smoke. The side door was either locked, or stuck. Raymond took two steps back and ran, full force, into the door. It flew open and he pulled me outside." She looked at him, and then turned to Jonny. "He saved both our lives."

"I watched Arthur Collins and Richard Holmes drive away from the scene," Elijah said. "I believed at the time they didn't realize Raymond and Martha had escaped. More important, they had no idea I had witnessed the entire thing."

"I was concerned about Raymond's well-being, and he was concerned about me," Martha said.

"Her face was smoke-smudged. I told her she needed to go home, right then," Raymond said. "I was okay, just a bruised shoulder. I asked her if she had any idea who would have done this."

Martha said, "I was out of breath, and I had a small abrasion on my right forearm. I told him it could be anyone." She paused for a moment. "He put his hands on my shoulders, right there on Stuart Street. All he could do was apologize to me, as if any of this was his fault. He worried about the fire destroying the newspaper building and was concerned about the Dellinger family. That's the kind of man your grandfather was, even back then," she said, "worried about everyone but himself. He had no idea—none of us did—what was to come."

"All I knew at that moment was I was afraid, and I was exhausted," Raymond said. "I just wanted to get home."

Elijah said, "While they were both heading home, believing, I suppose that they were safe, I called the fire department. After I reported the fire, I called the sheriff's department. I told them who started the fire, that there were people in the building, and then I hung up the telephone. I drove around for about another half hour looking for Samuel, and when I couldn't find him downtown, I started for home."

Chapter 12

Jonquil was trying mightily to honor her grandfather's instruction to let them finish the story. She was unable to keep up with how many questions she had. She moved her eyes from one to the other as they spoke.

"I caught up with Collins and Holmes at the Gulf station near the north edge of town," Elijah said. "I watched Holmes jump out of Collins's truck and make a phone call. Sam, I guess. I couldn't hear the conversation, but it appeared to me he was excited. They pulled off to the side and just sat there for a while. Not sure why." He turned to Raymond. "You remember where you went after you left the newspaper office?"

"I do," said Raymond. "I ran, full tilt, all the way up Stuart to where it crosses the pike, and then just started walking. Today, I could probably hitch a ride like Jonny sometimes does, but back then, even in uniform, I doubt anyone 'cept for another colored would have picked me up."

The three of them stopped talking long enough to drink some water. Jonny did wonder, for a moment, what they all were thinking now about what they all had done and seen. What memories had she stirred up after all this time? What regrets?

"Well," Elijah said, picking up where he'd left off, "seems like they left maybe ten, fifteen minutes later. Arthur drove and Richard rode shotgun. Both of them were sure they'd gotten away with what they'd done until Richard pointed out his window at someone walking slowly along the east side of the pike.

"Arthur slowed the truck. They stopped behind Raymond. Looked to me—I was maybe a hundred yards behind them—that Raymond was trying to catch his breath. He was stopped, standing on the shoulder of the road.

"I saw Arthur grab his gun, looked like a .22 rifle, from the rack in his truck. Raymond, you must have heard them coming because I saw you turn and look right at Arthur."

"Yeah, I did. Heard the bastard say something like 'This gonna be a bad time for this nigger,' and then he slammed the butt of the rifle into my forehead. The two of them picked me up and tossed me into the truck bed like I was a bag of damn dirt."

"It was getting dark," Elijah said. "I stayed behind them, cut my lights, and headed north. I was prepared to follow them wherever these two brainless idiots were going, but I was pretty sure I didn't have far to go. I kept my distance, driving with my lights off until I saw Collins' truck turn at the long driveway leading up to what was then my brother's place. 'My God,' I thought. When I was certain I wouldn't be noticed, I coasted past the house. When I was a few hundred yards past, I floored it so as to get to my own place a mile further up the pike. I pulled into my driveway, left the truck idling, jumped out, and went to my garage. I turned the combination lock on my gun safe already knowing what I wanted. Without a second thought, I grabbed an M1903 Springfield and two five-shot magazines filled with thirty ought six rounds."

Elijah took a moment and explained he'd bought the old long gun two years after returning from US Army service. He'd been one of a handful of army and Marine Corps snipers deployed to eliminate specific high-value North Korean targets from great distances. It wasn't something he was proud of, but it was work he learned to do well. "I never talk much about what I did during the war, but I had a firearms instructor, a black NCO from New York City, who helped develop me into the military asset I ultimately became. His name was Master Sergeant Selman Haynes. He died following a stroke a year and a half after he retired, back in 1956. I made the only trip north I ever would, to a black church in the Bronx in New York City, to pay respects to the man who'd helped me realize the folly of the prejudices I'd been raised with.

"I prayed I wouldn't have to kill anyone that night.

I hoped I could rely on what I'd learned years earlier from a steady-handed mentor."

Raymond nodded. Martha dabbed at her eyes. Jonny sat, stoic. One by one, her questions were getting answered.

"I guess I'll take it from here for a bit," Raymond said. "I was never unconscious. When they stopped, I looked up and saw Sam Hampton staring into the bed of the truck. He just shook his head and said he was glad his daddy wasn't alive to see what a mess Collins and Holmes made of what should have been a simple firebombing. That's what he said, a simple firebombing." He looked at Elijah. "He complained about your daddy hiring my people to work his land. Said he would never understand it.

"I asked Sam what was going on," Raymond said. "Next thing I knew Richard Holmes was pointing his .22 at me. Sam told me I should already be dead, then he asked them about you, Martha." Raymond chuckled at the memory. "Collins said, 'Guess she walked away, too.' My God but those boys were some ignorant—"

"Careful, Raymond," Martha said. "Young ears over there." She pointed at Jonny, who smiled.

"I've heard most of those words before," Jonny said.

"What did you have to say to that, Raymond," Elijah asked.

"I said something like 'Guess you clowns wasn't near as smart as you thought.' Maybe something else, like 'redneck assholes' or something like that. Anyway,

Collins raised his rifle and worked a round into the chamber. Sam waved him off. Scared the daylights out of me when he told Arthur not to waste a bullet on me but to get a rope."

"I'm guessing somewhere around that time," Elijah said, "I parked my truck off the shoulder of the pike behind a clump of waste weeds and shrubs grown high enough to offer some cover from passing cars and trucks. I'd only brought two magazines for the Springfield; I was pretty sure I wouldn't need more than two or three rounds unless I had failed to correctly assess the situation. I was also pretty sure I understood what those young idiots were considering. I knew my brother well enough to know that lynching had not yet been relegated to the trash heap of history in Samuel's worldview. In any case, I didn't plan on letting those three do what I was thinking they had in mind.

"I made my way through the woods, walking as close to the road as was safe. I needed to stay invisible to passing traffic. By then, it was well after nine. It was dark but the path was sufficiently starlit for me to stay on course. I prayed I wasn't too late, and I hoped I'd maintained enough of my military training to do what needed to be done. I also prayed you was in as good a shape as you would need to be in order to make it through.

"That nasty old oak behind the house provided only a single, small line of sight from where I was perched. I watched things unfold from nearly a quarter mile away. I used a pair of powerful, military-grade field glasses. My first look told me I was right about what they were going to do. Those idiots had a lynching on their minds."

Jonny and the others paid rapt attention to Elijah's words. He told them there was no misinterpreting the rope over the thick horizontal branch nearly twelve feet off the ground. Raymond was still on the ground with his hands tied behind his back and his feet trussed at the ankles.

"I put the glasses down and sighted the scene through the scope on my Springfield. Due to my training, I knew I could end things quickly simply by killing my idiot brother and those two other pieces of garbage. I didn't dwell on the moral implications, but I did momentarily consider doing just that. Then I figured if they truly were the ignorant cowards I believed them to be, there was a better way that, in the end, would constitute more appropriate punishment."

Raymond said, "I remember saying 'You don't have to do this, Mr. Sam. The world's changing, and you can become a man of the future instead of one still living in the past.' He didn't pay me no mind.

"He said, 'Will one of you gag that son of a bitch. I don't give a rat's ass what's changing. Niggers don't get with white women in my town. Not now, not ever! You hear me?' He was gonna do what he was gonna do.

"Richard Holmes pushed some wadded-up paper into my mouth. I wished I could have explained what

Martha and I were doing. You know, moving a file cabinet from one place to another in the front room of the *Clarion*'s offices, but it wouldn't have mattered. These three were raised with ideas that people like me were something less than human.

"I watched Arthur Collins. He was making a noose. I watched him do it. It was scary. He had no hesitation; he knew exactly what he was doing. He put it around my neck. Then the three of them carried me over to a footstool Sam had placed under the tree limb. Sam and Richard Holmes stood me onto the stool. Collins tightened the noose around my neck. They started talking about what they would do after they kicked the stool out from under me. All I could do was watch 'em and listen.

"Sam told them they needed to get this done and then get to the old Melton Roadhouse over in Taylor County. He said something like, 'I'll 'discover' this when the two of you drop me off, later on.' Sam lifted me by my legs. The other two tied the rope around the trunk of the tree. Sam let go of my legs. They landed on the stool. I started in on the Lord's Prayer, just kept sayin' it, over and over. They couldn't make it out, 'cause of the paper in my mouth.

"Sam said, 'Soon as I kick this stool out, we'll get out of here. I'll meet you at the truck. Go on, get going!' Saw Holmes spit on the ground in front of the stool. Then, Holmes and Collins walked to Collins's truck. Sam walked around the stool two or three times.

Then, he said, 'You know, I told my daddy we didn't need no nigger sharecroppers. And we damn sure don't need niggers doing none of our women 'round here. You're gonna be a message to every damn nigger between here and Oxford.' Then, he kicked the stool. He watched me fight the noose. That's 'bout the last thing I remember."

Silent tears flowed from Martha and Jonny's eyes. Elijah had his head down. Raymond stared at the wall in front of his bed. Elijah exhaled a long breath.

"I guess this is my part," he said. "I was flat on the ground, prone, looking through the scope on my rifle. I watched my brother kick the stool, turn, and run toward Arthur Collins's truck. Soon as he got into the cab, Collins turned the truck around and floored it. When he got to the pike, he turned north, toward Taylor County. I turned back to check on Raymond. I sighted on his head, then straight up, onto the rope itself. I knew waiting was dangerous, but I needed the rope to be still before I could shoot at it.

"I guess it was maybe forty-five seconds before you lost consciousness.

"I remember, I whispered, 'Stop fighting, Raymond.' Soon as you were still, I took my first shot. It cut the rope, but not entirely. Second shot did the job. I watched you drop to the ground. I guess the fall was only about two, two-and-a-half feet. Soon as I saw you fall, I ran, full tilt, nonstop. It felt like it took forever, but it was probably only ninety seconds at the most. I dropped to my knees, loosened the noose, and began checking you out. You were bleeding from cuts on your neck, caused by the noose, I suppose. But you were breathing. I remember saying, 'Come on, come on, Raymond. You can do this.'

"You started wheezing and coughing. You opened your eyes and immediately started shakin' your head. You kept sayin' no, no, no. I cut the rope around your ankles. Then, when you settled down, I cut the rope around your wrists. I guess by then you realized it was me and not Samuel, because you said my name."

"I did," Raymond said. "Then, I started to tell you it was your brother who did this, and you said, 'Yeah, I know. And Arthur Collins and Richard Holmes.' I think I started crying right about then."

"I had to talk you out of going to police," Elijah said.

"Yeah, I remember that. You told me they'd figure out a way to make it my fault," Raymond said.

Jonny couldn't take it anymore. "Make it your fault? How was any of this your fault? That's crazy."

All three of the grown-ups smiled.

"I know you can't imagine it, but that's the way things were back then, Jonquil," Martha said. "If Raymond had gone to the police . . . I guess it would have been the county sheriff's office . . . they'd probably have arrested him for trespassing."

"That is just plain stupid," Jonny said. "I mean, didn't you live on that property?"

Raymond nodded. "Yes, I did."

"I told your grandfather," Elijah said, "while we were standing there in the dark, a few minutes after he'd almost died . . . been murdered . . . that Collins and Holmes would be arrested the following morning for the firebombing at the newspaper office. I also told him, pretty much, how things would play out from there." Elijah looked at Raymond. "When I told you how the fire happened, you just looked at me and said, 'You know about that?'"

"That was when I heard that Elijah knew those two started the fire," Raymond said.

"I didn't know about that until Mr. Dellinger called our house and told my mother what had happened," Martha said.

Elijah said, "Then I told Raymond, 'I know I have no right to expect anything from you, but you need to trust me. This is still Mississippi. You're still colored. They're still white. Your family sharecrops. Their families have been landowners here for generations.'"

Martha cocked her head to one side and looked intently at Elijah. "You know, listening to this, it seems you could have stopped it all from happening," she said.

"Oh, don't think I haven't thought about that over the years, Martha," Elijah said. "I also could have gotten shot for my trouble if I'd interfered at the newspaper office, and then I might not have been around for the business at Samuel's house."

"I asked him the same question that night," Raymond said, "after he saved my life. You remember what you told me?"

"I told you if I rolled in on them while they were getting ready to lynch you—you know, it's still hard to even say that word—that Richard Holmes or Arthur Collins or my own brother, for that matter, might have just shot both of us and staged the scene to look like you and I had some kind of shootout. It wouldn't have taken much."

Raymond nodded. "All these years later ain't no time for second guessing what turned out okay at the time," he said. He looked at Martha, then at Jonny. "I'll tell you how crazy it was. I reminded Elijah that my daddy and mama had gone to his daddy's funeral when he passed, a year or two earlier. Remember what you said?"

Elijah nodded. "Think I told you that my daddy was fine with your people working for him, but you weren't ever gonna be invited to Sunday dinner."

"Well," Martha said, "I'd have invited you over for Sunday dinner, Raymond."

"Uh-huh," Raymond said. "I'm not so sure your mama would have been too happy with that." He looked at Elijah. "I just wanted to go home. You asked me if me or my daddy had a gun, remember that?"

"That's right," Elijah said. "You didn't say anything, as I recall."

"I didn't say nothin' 'cause it was illegal for blacks to have guns in Pitts County back then," he said. "Guess we had a couple."

"I just wanted to make sure they could protect themselves once Samuel realized Raymond was alive and their plan didn't work," Elijah said.

"I didn't know anything about what happened after that," Raymond said. "I went home." He turned to Jonny. "We were in that little house down by the creek back then."

"I told you how things would play out the next day," Elijah said. "I was right."

Elijah told them how Collins and Holmes were arrested based on his anonymous tip and how they were ultimately tried and convicted and spent eight years at Parchman Farm. He also told them all how his brother's own fate occurred. Even now, neither Raymond nor Martha knew anything about that.

Raymond said, "I remember you told me you were gonna have a . . . what did you call it? A personal man-to-man, heart-to-heart conversation with Sam." Raymond laughed. "I got that right?"

"Yes, you do. And yes, I did."

Chapter 13

"My brother and I were named for Old Testament prophets," Elijah said. "One of the prophet Samuel's roles was as a judge. Elijah, among other things, was said to have worked miracles. It turned out a little like that with us. My daddy always told my brother, 'If you smart, you'll read your Bible, you'll pay attention while you in school, you'll listen to your daddy and to your big brother, and you'll do okay, boy.' No matter how many times he said it, Samuel never could quite get it right."

Jonny and the others took a break from the story of May 26, 1960 for some snacks and soft drinks. In Raymond's case, it meant a bag of pretzels and a glass of water.

"Maybe," Martha said, "we should get the rest of this story tomorrow, when everyone has had time to rest, and Raymond can have another good night's sleep."

Jonny vetoed that idea, most respectfully. "How can anyone sleep without knowing what happened with Sam Hampton?" she asked. Then she remembered she hadn't factored everyone else's age, but Elijah said he was fine, and Raymond was euphoric being alive and with the three living people he cared about most in the world.

"As a child, Sam followed me around like a puppy," Elijah said. "I was nine years older. I was big, strong, a natural leader, my daddy said. By the time Sam turned eleven years old, our mother had left, tired of being treated, at best, like furniture by our daddy. At worst, when he was drunk, my mama was a convenient target for Jethro's fists and feet. When she'd had enough, she waited for an opening, packed a single bag, walked up that long gravel driveway to the pike, and put her thumb out. No one in Pitts County, including the three of us, saw or heard from her after that day.

"The other loss in Samuel's life occurred when I was drafted into the army and sent to fight in Korea. This left the boy in the sole custody of his father, who, as I said, was a nasty drunk. Samuel was crushed.

"Before he died," Elijah said, "my granddaddy, his name was Joshua Hampton, carved up the family's holdings. He left his home and property to Jethro but parceled out a sizable piece a mile up the Pitts Taylor Pike and placed it in a trust for me, to be put into my name when I turned twenty-one. I turned twenty-one while I was in the army, but the papers had been filed, and the property became mine when I returned to Vosalia in 1953. I came home from Korea when I was twenty-two years old."

"Tell us what happened when you had your personal conversation with Samuel," Jonny said. Elijah looked at Raymond, then Martha. Raymond nodded.

"It was a little after ten on the morning after Sam, Arthur Collins, and Richard Holmes attempted to lynch your grandfather for being a black man seen in public in the company of a white woman. Sam woke up on the floor of his living room with me standing over him, pointing a 12-gauge at his head." Raymond smiled at the image.

"I told him, 'There's a cup of hot, black coffee on the side table there, Samuel. Get your drunk sorry ass up off the floor and swallow some of it down.' Right then, if my gun had accidentally gone off, I probably would have burned the house down with his worthless body inside. I'm not proud about that but it's the truth. He tried but his body wasn't ready for him to stand up. The best he could do was sit there with his back up against the front of the sofa and his legs out in front of him.

"None of you would have any way of knowing this but our lives were, for several years, as separate as possible, with us living in houses a mile apart on the Pitts Taylor Pike. But old habits and tight family ties were pretty strong. When it was me talking to him, Samuel turned into a small, needy, nearly helpless child. It took him a few moments but as soon as he became aware of his surroundings and circumstances, he started crying like a baby.

"I told him, 'You can cry all you want to, Samuel, but here's some truth for you to chew on; I know everything, and I mean *everything* that happened yesterday.'"

"What did he have to say to that?" Martha asked.

"Oh, you know, lying, making excuses. 'I don't know what you're talking about,' that kind of bullshit."

"He didn't have any idea, did he?" Raymond said.

"None. 'Samuel!' I shouted. 'Everything! I know you and those two ignorant moron friends of yours are responsible for what happened at the newspaper. I know what the three of you tried to do to your sharecropper's son last night. I know the three of you disappeared up to that roadhouse over in Taylor County, and I know they dumped your drunk, sorry ass out at the driveway at two o'clock in the morning so you could crawl on your hands and knees back home like the worthless reptile you are.'"

"Wow!" Jonny said. "You called your brother a reptile? That is harsh."

"He didn't deserve anything but harsh, Jonquil," Elijah said. "He still was in that state of denial, though. I told him, 'Be smart, Samuel, and just listen so I don't have to either repeat myself or blow your damn head off and bury you out back with the dogs. I watched the three of you, all damn night. Your friends?' I told him, 'They're already in the county jail, charged with arson and a whole shitload of other crimes. And they're probably trying to blame each other and probably trying to blame you for trying to kill those two people at the newspaper office.'

"All that stupid, pathetic excuse for a man could come up with was, 'He was with a white woman, Elijah! What were we supposed to do?' Can you believe that shit? I told him, 'You were supposed to mind your own goddam business.' I said, 'That's what you were supposed to do. I know Daddy poisoned your head, Samuel, but you helping them start a fire at the newspaper and then trying to lynch someone who works for you? You are at least a dozen different kinds of stupid, Samuel.'

"Samuel managed to get to his feet, and immediately he stumbled backward, missed the sofa completely, and knocked over the table with the cup of coffee I had brought to him. He stayed down on the floor, crying, waiting. I put the shotgun down on the rug in front of the fireplace. I picked him up by the back of his neck and sat him in a chair. He looked at me. Hell, I don't know what was going on in that fool empty head of his. Sobriety hadn't quite arrived, but I'm pretty sure he knew who, what, and where he was and was just waiting for what he knew was coming.

"I said to him, 'You know, I told Daddy not to leave you this land and this house. You don't have any idea how to run a farm, even one you don't have to work your own self. And look how you take care of this place. Animals live better and cleaner than this.' I guess I gave him a dose of medicine he should have gotten years earlier.

"He tried getting to his feet again, but his stomach had other ideas. He threw up nearly everything he'd eaten and drank the day before. I moved out of the way and watched. When he finished, I just stood there and shook my head. I lowered my voice and let what little might have been left of brotherly love come out.

"I said, 'Samuel, pay attention to me. You do exactly what I tell you and maybe, just maybe, you'll get through this stupid, crazy, awful thing you have done without spending years of your life in jail.'

"All this idiot could say to me was, 'I didn't do nothin', Elijah. You don't know nothin' and I ain't done nothin.'"

Raymond had an amused look on his face. "I don't think I ever heard you talk to anyone like that, Elijah," he said.

"Oh, I talked to this damn fool like that all the time. No way you'd know any of that, Raymond," Elijah said. "I couldn't believe how just plain stupid my brother was.

"I summoned up all my patience. 'Samuel,' I said, 'did you not hear what I just said? I saw *everything*. I saw, with my own eyes, your two friends firebomb the newspaper office. I know why they did that. I know Raymond, your sharecropper's son, was in the newspaper office with a white girl, Martha Plemmons.' I told him all of this. 'I'm the one called the fire service and the Pitts County sheriff. I watched Collins and Holmes pick that soldier up off the pike and bring him here. I watched everything. I watched you play judge—those two lowlifes were your damn jury—and I watched all three of you try to be his executioner. After you all drove away last night, I saved that man's life. Me! I saw all of it, every blessed damn second of it!' Then, I picked up the shotgun and held it in my right hand.

"He was outraged. 'Why'd you save his goddam life, Elijah? You care more 'bout some nigger than you care about me, your own flesh and blood? About your own people?' Then, the fool tried to blame it all on me."

"He said, 'This is all your fault, Elijah. If you hadn't left, if you hadn't gone off to kill gooks somewhere halfway round the world . . . gooks . . . Why'd you have to leave, Elijah? Why?'

"'I was drafted, you idiot,' I said. 'You think I wanted to go over there?' I honestly didn't know what else to say to him.

"Then he goes and gets all pitiful on me. 'What am I gonna do, Elijah? First Mama left, then you. Daddy was drunk all the time and mean and none of this would have happened if you didn't leave, Elijah!'

"I grabbed him by his arm and dragged him into the kitchen, away from the stink of his vomit. I heated up whatever was left in the old silver percolator I'd filled with coffee before I woke his sorry ass up. We sat at the kitchen table with fresh cups. Neither of us said a word. I stared at him. He avoided looking at me.

"'Samuel,' I said, 'with you, everything that happens is always someone else's damn fault. There's only one way out of this for you, but you have to listen, and you have to do exactly and only what I tell you. If you don't, I promise, I will drive to the Pitts County sheriff's office and tell them everything I saw last night, and all three of you will spend the rest of your worthless lives down at Parchman. What you did was just plain wrong, and there's no southern or Confederate bullshit you can shovel can justify trying to kill someone just because you don't like the color of his skin.'"

Jonny looked at Elijah with deep, newfound admiration and respect. Martha and Raymond just looked at each other. The night nurse came into Raymond's room.

"I need for you folks to let Mr. Steadman get his rest. Visiting hours end in about thirty minutes," she said.

"Ma'am," Jonny said, "we need to be here for a little while longer. I promise, my grandfather will sleep like a baby tonight."

"What you talkin' about, girl?" Raymond said.

Jonny said, softly, "My guess? You've been carrying all this for way too long, Poppop."

"Amen to that, Jonquil," Martha said. "Amen, darling."

"Okay," the nurse said, "but next time I come in, you all need to head on out, you hear?"

"I'll be right here," Jonny said, "right in this chair." The nurse nodded and left. Martha and Elijah looked at Jonny and smiled.

"You are certainly becoming quite the young lady, Jonquil," Elijah said. "Now, where was I?"

"I think you were having that come-to-Jesus conversation with Samuel, Elijah," Martha said.

He nodded. "Oh, yeah, that's right. Okay. I had nothing left in me but simple human reason," Elijah said. "I told him, 'As of now, nobody knows anything about what happened here last night except five people—you, me, Raymond, Arthur Collins, and Richard Holmes. It is in absolutely no one's interest for anyone to say anything about that. I won't, and I believe Raymond won't even though he probably should.' Samuel was looking at me and he actually seemed to be listening.

"'I know you didn't throw anything at the newspaper office yesterday, but you got those two pieces of shit all riled up to do that 'cause you didn't like that young colored man talking to that young white woman. Period. They may try to put it off on you, but all you have to do is say you didn't know nothing about it until you heard about it today, from me. I'll verify that if I have to.'"

"You told him you would do that?" Raymond asked.

"He asked me if I meant it. I had something

important I wanted—no, I needed from him," Elijah said. "This was what I was referring to when I asked you to trust me. You remember me asking you to trust me?"

Raymond nodded. "I do, Elijah."

"I told him, 'You are ignorant, and you did something really bad and really wrong, Samuel, but for better or worse you are still my brother. Until I have children or, God help us, until you have children, we are all that's left of the Hampton family in this place. So, yes,' I told him, 'I'll do that for you, but I want you to make a plan, down the road a bit, to leave Vosalia, leave Pitts County, and I want you to do the right thing by those people down there.' I pointed in the direction of the small house by Taylor Creek where you and your family lived.

"I told him once Holmes and Collins got what was coming to them, I'd give him a year, or two, to find someplace else to live, something else to do with his miserable life, and then he needed to deed his property to the people been working it for all those years. I told him that, but I knew he wouldn't give up without a fight. "He said, 'Why I gotta do that, Elijah? Those people never did nothing for me.' I just shook my head at him."

"'Those people,' I said, 'been doing all the work on the farm and been putting food in your mouth and money in your pocket since Daddy died. You haven't done a damn thing for yourself. That's the deal, Samuel. It'll damn sure be a miracle if it works, but that's the deal. You do this, I'll protect you. You don't? I won't. And that means you join your friends down at Parchman Farm.'

"I just stared into his eyes. Maybe a minute, maybe two minutes passed before Samuel nodded his empty head and took the deal."

Jonquil took a few moments to digest the feast of information she'd been served. As Martha and Raymond regarded one another, Jonny's eyes flitted back and forth from one of them to the other. She wasn't sure what, if anything, to say.

At that moment she finally took note of her grandfather's neck. In the hospital gown, absent the turtle necked shirts he always wore, she was able to see the remnants of the damage the noose had done more than a half-century earlier. She walked to his bedside and touched his neck. He managed a tired smile.

"You see?"

She nodded. Martha snatched a tissue from the box on Raymond's meal table and dabbed at her tears.

"They started that fire because you talked to each other?" Jonny said.

"The ignorance and the hatred ran so deep," Martha said between sobs. "Passed down from generation to generation. I told you all about that the first time we met and talked. Do you remember? I'm sad to say some of it is still the same today."

Jonny touched the bandage over her eyebrow. "Yeah, about that." She picked this moment to tell the three of them the real story behind her injuries.

Raymond erupted. "It's 'cause of that damn history paper," he said. "When I get outta here—"

"When you get out of here," Jonny said, "you're gonna be on an Oreo-free diet for the rest of your cranky, grumpy life, old man." She softened and reached for his hand. "You don't have anything to worry about. Those boys are going to think twice before they come at me again. I got my licks in, Poppop."

Martha Plemmons looked a question at Jonny. "One of those miserable bastards—oh, I'm so sorry, Jonquil. I don't typically employ such low language. Anyway, one of those . . . I don't even know what to call them—wasn't one of them named Holmes?"

"Yes," Jonny said. "Fred Holmes. His grandfather, Richard, and Arthur Collins were the ones who burned down the newspaper office. It's probably because he knows I plan to include that in my paper that he and his chump friends came after me. Now, I get to include everything that happened after the fire." They sat quietly for a moment.

Jonny's eyes widened and her mouth fell open. "That's it! That's it!"

"That's what, Jonquil?" Raymond asked.

"That's what *didn't* happen on May 26, 1960!" she said.

Martha and Raymond shared a skeptical glance. "What you mean, that's what didn't happen?" Raymond said. "A whole lot happened!"

"The lynching," she said, smiling. "The lynching didn't happen! They tried; it was supposed to happen, but it didn't happen!"

Raymond couldn't help breaking into a smile, followed by robust laughter. "Martha, you two talked at some length, what, twice? She tell you about the talking tree?"

Jonny put her hands on her hips. "Poppop!"

"No, Raymond, you mentioned it, but I'd love to hear about it from Jonquil."

He smiled at his granddaughter. "Come on now, Jonny. We're all sharing here this evening, aren't we?"

Jonny sent a pained look at Martha Plemmons. Martha smiled expectantly.

"I'm sorry, Martha, uh, Miss Plemmons," Jonny she said, directing her eyes to Raymond. Martha smiled again. Jonny went through her two experiences having fallen asleep under the old, dying oak in the backyard. She explained how, the first time, she dreamed the tree gave her the date, May 26, 1960, and told her "but it didn't happen."

"The second dream, the tree apologized for what it did but repeated that it didn't happen," she said. "I thought it was strange myself, but after everyone tried to talk me into writing about something else, it led me to look into the fire at the newspaper, which I now know was connected to the lynching even though the lynching didn't happen." She looked at Raymond, smiled, and nodded once.

"You happy now, old man?" she asked. "Now I look like a crazy person in front of Miss Plemmons. Excuse me. Martha." She turned her eyes to Martha. "I know what it sounds like but it's what happened. I promise."

Martha put both her hands out to Jonny. She gripped Jonny's hands tightly. "There is nothing either stupid or crazy about our dreams, Jonquil," she said, staring into the young girl's eyes. "Dreams are sometimes confused and cluttered and contain all sorts of seemingly disconnected bits and pieces of random information, but they often help us make sense of things we might not fully understand. And," she said, "dreams sometimes actually predict things yet to occur. I am a very big believer in dreams, Jonquil." She looked at Raymond. "You listen to me, Turtle," she said. "Don't you dare dismiss or make fun of your granddaughter's dreams. Sometimes," she turned her gaze to Jonny, "they're all we have to cling to and hold onto."

"Excuse me, but I've got a question," Jonny said.

"Big surprise," Raymond said. "You always got some question or another, right? I guess you waited long enough. What you got for me, Jonquil?"

She said nothing but instead looked across at her grandfather. He looked a question at her.

"What you doin' girl? Spit it out."

"Okay, okay. After, you know, that . . . night when those yahoos . . ."

"Yeah, yeah, yeah, I remember it. I was there. What about it?"

"Did you ever see Sam Hampton again? You were living down by the creek, right? He was living up in the big house. Did you ever see him?"

He glanced at Elijah. "Look here," Raymond said. "I kept a very low profile after that night and before I left for Germany. No, I didn't see Sam Hampton then. In fact, I didn't see him ever again, Jonny. 'Sides, Elijah told me it'd be better all around, for everyone, if nothin' else happened between the Steadman family and the Hampton family, 'cept with him, that is, 'till after everything with the fire at the newspaper played out with the police and, if it ever got to that, in court."

"So, you went to Germany and your parents . . ."

"Jonny, my parents both went to their graves not ever knowing everything that happened that night other than I got into a scuffle with some rednecks on my way home from town. It was like Elijah said, nothing good would've come from telling them anything. I was going to Germany, and they had to continue to sharecrop at least till I got back home. Sam damn sure wasn't gonna say nothin,' and 'sides, most of their dealings—my parents—were with Elijah after that night."

"Actually," Elijah said, "there's some stuff in the

aftermath of all that bad shit—sorry, all that happened—I'm not entirely sure you know about, Raymond."

Raymond raised his eyebrows and looked at his friend. "What exactly don't I know, Elijah?"

Elijah smiled. "It's nothin' bad, Turtle." Elijah went on to share the fact that he had his brother move in with him and his wife after that morning meeting of the minds they'd had.

"I just thought it'd be better if you and your folks didn't have to have anything to do with him anymore," he said. "I'd already told him that his freedom was directly linked to keeping me happy, and that I'd be happy if he didn't set foot on that property ever again. I moved whatever he was gonna need into a spare room in my house and let him know that for the foreseeable future, he was working for me."

"What you tellin' me, Elijah?" Raymond asked. "That house was, what, empty till you gave it over to my folks?"

Elijah sat, stoic, before turning his attention to Jonquil.

"None of it matters anymore, but your granddaddy here didn't know this." He turned to Raymond. "Yes, it was empty, Turtle. I didn't know what you did and didn't tell your people about what happened, and I didn't want to stir anything up until everything was said and done and Samuel was gone for good."

Raymond looked at him for a moment, nodded his

head twice, and then turned his attention to Jonny. "You got anything else?"

She nodded her head. She wasn't quite done. "I just want to understand it all," she said. "The thing is, except for that stuff with those three idiot boys, I don't see a whole lot of that racist stuff in my life. It really bothers me to know you had to live with all that."

All three of the grownups nodded and looked at one another.

"It's good that you don't see a whole lot of it, Jonny," Raymond said. "I suspect it's 'cause you who you are—a great student, great person, a great athlete—that sort of stuff. But there's still a whole lot of history between white people and black people, and I'm sorry, but as you grow up and live your life and encounter people . . ."

Elijah shook his head. Martha sighed.

"I know what you're saying, Poppop," Jonny said.

"I wish it was different, Jonny," Raymond said, "but a whole lotta minds gotta do a whole lotta changin' 'fore this stuff is behind us. Maybe someday . . ."

Jonny looked at Martha. "Okay, last question, maybe. Why do you and Mr. Belvoir and Mr. Hampton all call him Turtle?" she asked. "Is it because he wears those dumb shirts to hide those scars on his neck?"

Martha looked at her and Raymond's hands.

"I said something to your grandfather a long time ago, Jonquil," she said. "I'm afraid it was . . . perhaps something I shouldn't have said." She looked at Raymond. "Do you mind?"

He smiled at Martha. "You were right, what you said to me back then. I was still shaken from everything that happened. I was also young and stupid and . . . no, I don't mind, Martha. After all that's happened and all this time, hell, we told her everything else, might as well go and put a ribbon around it. Jonquil, go and tell that nurse that we gonna be here a few minutes longer."

Elijah stood and stretched. "I'll tell her. I need to get myself back home before they check me in here for bein' old, tired, and stupid." He put his hand on Raymond's. "No more Oreos, Mr. Steadman." He and Martha hugged. He whispered, "I'm glad you're here, Martha. I'm not sure he'd have talked about this if you weren't."

"Good night, Elijah," she said. "And thank you for everything. Then and now."

Elijah looked at Jonny. "I'm sure I'll be seeing you again, Jonquil. Maybe soon."

"You can count on it, Mr. Hampton," she said, and gave him a long, quiet hug.

CHAPTER 14

Jonny sat down in the green vinyl chair. She looked expectantly at Martha. Raymond nodded his head. "Go ahead, Martha. Guess she needs to hear this also."

"It was two or three days later," she said, "after the fire and . . . what happened to your grandfather later that evening. I can't bring myself to use that disgusting word."

"It was what it was, Martha," he said. "They tried to lynch me. Woulda done it, too, but for Elijah."

Martha swallowed hard, shook her head, and sat up in her chair. "In one way, it wasn't a matter of such importance," she said.

"It must have been something," Jonny said. "You have trouble talking about it."

"Oh, Jonquil," Martha said. Tears started pouring out of her eyes. "Sometimes we say things to people when our emotions take over from our sense of reason."

Jonny took a second to glance at her grandfather.

He was fighting to keep his own composure. She looked back at Martha. "All this . . . it's about you and the others calling him Turtle?"

Martha regained her calm. "No, Jonquil, it's much more than that." She smiled. "We, your grandfather and I, saw each other down on South Street a few days after what happened," she said. "I was with my mother. We'd just come from a late breakfast with Mr. Dellinger to talk about how the paper would work in the wake of the fire and all the damage it caused."

"I was there to pick up a tool at a hardware store over across the tracks," Raymond said. "I wasn't in uniform. Just wearing a pair of work pants and a pullover shirt, one of those turtlenecks you love so much. Was walking to my father's truck when I spotted her across the street. Should have kept my head down and not let her see me."

"Oh, fiddle faddle, Raymond," she said. "You looked just fine, quite good, in fact." Jonny and Raymond both chuckled. "I guess I've been saying that all my life. Anyway, I saw him, he saw me, and I told my mother I'd be right back. I ran across the street."

"Weren't you afraid?" Jonny asked her. "I mean, look what happened the last time people saw the two of you talking to each other."

"I don't think either one of us cared about that," Raymond said. "We'd been through something together and hadn't spoken about it with each other."

"Oh, I didn't care, even a little bit," Martha said.

"Anyway, I ran across the street and didn't even think about any of that. I saw him. And I hugged him." If defiance had a particular expression, Jonny saw it on Martha's face.

He smiled at her and at Jonny. "I'm here to report that I did not hug that pretty young white woman back," he said. "I was painfully aware of what was happening right then and right there and was, you'll pardon me, Miss Plemmons, scared for my life and yours. I was scared out of my own wits, if I ever even had any of those."

"I asked him if he was okay," she said. "He just nodded and asked me the same question. I told him I was fine. He looked around; there were a few people, but it didn't appear anyone, except perhaps for my mother, was paying any mind to us."

Raymond took a drink of water. Martha asked Jonny to pour her a cup.

"Your mother saw all of this?" Jonny asked.

"Oh, heavens, yes," Martha said. "We had a long talk about it later, when I returned home."

"One of these days," Raymond said, "you're gonna tell me about that conversation, Miss Plemmons."

Martha presented him with a radiant smile. "Maybe I will and maybe I won't, Mr. Steadman. Anyway"—she turned back to Jonny— "he told me what happened later that evening when he was almost—I don't mind telling you, Jonquil, I was mortified. I started apologizing and apologizing, but he told me it wasn't my fault, and we kind of fussed over one another for a few moments."

Everyone was quiet for a bit.

"I could see how that would be a hard thing to talk about, especially back then," Jonny said. "But where does Turtle come in?"

"Your grandfather told me that we shouldn't be talking to one another, especially right there on South Street, in front of God and the whole world." She looked at him. "Do you remember what you said to me?"

A sadness came to his eyes. He took in a deep breath and let it out, slowly. "I've never forgotten a single word of it," he said.

"Nor have I, Raymond," she said.

Jonny was fidgeting in her seat. "Will one of you please tell me?"

"Okay, dear," Martha said. "Your grandfather told me we needed to not talk to one another anymore and not be seen together. He said he was leaving for Germany in a few days, had work to finish, and didn't have time for anything else."

"You gotta understand, Jonny." Raymond said. "I was still a very young man. I told Martha that I was going to be very careful who I spoke with, who I was seen with, who I let get anywhere close to me—in Vosalia, in Pitts County, in Mississippi, or anyplace in the United States of America or around the world," Raymond said. "I told her I was afraid of what people would do because I'd seen, up close and very personal, what almost happened to us and to me, just for being a black man talking to a white woman."

Martha took his hand and kissed it. She looked at Jonny.

"We were both young, Jonquil," she said. "That world, our world, was a different place then than it is now, although as you yourself have borne witness, there's still ignorance and hatred. I fear there always will be."

"I told her when Elijah saved my life that night, I decided I was not going to put myself or anyone I cared about in a position for that to happen again, if I could help it."

"And I told him that he might just as well be a turtle, who only feels safe inside its own shell and never lets anyone else get inside," Martha said. "I told him, right there on South Street, 'from now on, Corporal Steadman, your name is Turtle.' I walked across the street, took my mother by the arm, and we went home. I'm not sure exactly, because I knew he came home from time to time from the army, but I don't think I saw or heard from your grandfather for, I don't recall exactly, could it have been fifteen years?"

He nodded his head. "Could have been. We didn't write to one another, or any of that, and I couldn't bring myself to look her up for fear that things hadn't changed all that much in Vosalia," he said. "I did see Elijah Hampton from time to time, and the first time he called me Turtle, I realized that Martha must have gone ahead and renamed me, at least to him and probably to others."

They were still holding hands. Jonny smiled, moved closer, and put her own hand on top of theirs. "You two saw each other two times back in 1960," she said. "Once on May 26, then a couple days later." She looked from one to the other. "But you had feelings, right?"

"Well," Martha said, addressing Raymond, "I can't speak for Mr. Turtle over here, but yes, Jonquil, from virtually the moment we first met outside the *Clarion*, I had strong and very dangerous feelings for Corporal Raymond Steadman. And unless I really was incorrect and misinterpreted our brief encounter, I believe he reciprocated those feelings and took his leave of the situation out of a fear of anything else happening to me if we had decided to act on those feelings." She looked at him. "We've never talked about this, Raymond. Am I right?"

"Of course, you are, Martha. I'd be lying if I said I didn't feel something for you back then. Heck, I feel something for you right now! I've always felt something for you. But, where we were, where we are, there are people who just aren't ready for that."

Jonny turned her gaze to him, then her, back and forth. "You know, it's like I said. At school, in town, at the library, places like that, most people I know don't really care much about stuff like that anymore. Of course, there are a few losers who, I don't know, are just stupid and . . . you know, but mostly, it seems to me, people just don't care."

"*Mostly* being the issue, Jonny," Raymond said. "It only takes a few, or even just one, to create a whole bunch of problems."

Jonny knew first-hand; it only takes a couple of idiots. "Oh," she said, "before I forget, you said earlier, 'for the second time.' Are you telling me you told me all this before? I mean, I know a whole lot of stuff about you and about my relatives and all, but you never told me any of this before. What did you mean, 'for the second time'?"

Martha stood and grasped her walker. "I need to get home and get some sleep. All this talk and all this . . . time travel has simply worn me out." She walked to Raymond's bedside, bent down, and kissed him on the forehead. "I've missed you, Raymond," she said. She turned to Jonny. "Jonquil, would you please walk me outside? I need to find a ride home."

"I'll be right back, Poppop. Then, you can tell me." Jonny followed Martha out of Raymond's room.

"I'm glad we have a moment alone, Jonquil," Martha said. She took Jonny's hands in her own. "Tomorrow, or sometime very soon, you need to repeat your ritual down by that infernal tree."

Jonny gave her a beaming smile. "You believe me?"

"I believe something inspired you while you were napping down by that tree," she said. "And now that all of this, what should I call it, excavating of ancient memories, has happened, I think both of us and your grandfather would be interested in hearing if anything else magically flies into your very pretty, very perceptive head."

Jonny reached around her walker and gave Martha Plemmons another long, quiet hug. "I'm so happy the two of you got to visit tonight," she said. "I'll let you know if that dumb old tree has anything left for me."

A deputy from the Pitts County Sheriff's Department, who was at the hospital interviewing a witness to a traffic accident, offered to drive Martha home. Jonny went back to her grandfather's room, but he had already drifted off. She turned down the lights, curled herself up in the green vinyl-covered chair, pulled her iPad from her backpack, and began writing what she hoped would be the final draft of her "A" paper.

Two years into his tour in Germany, Raymond was overseeing an inventory of motor pool parts when he opened a letter from his father containing surprising news. Elijah Hampton had delivered a quitclaim deed to the entire eighty-two-acre property and to the house. Elijah had told Raymond's father that Sam had left Vosalia and was moving to Jacksonville, Florida. Since Elijah had said he had all he needed or wanted with his own property and farm, he'd convinced Sam to remember the people who had been doing all the work, and to deed the property over to Josiah and Constance Steadman.

Raymond asked his battalion commander for a week of leave he'd accumulated. His request was granted, and Sergeant Steadman returned to Vosalia to help his parents move into what they had always referred to as "the big house." For nearly fifteen years, until 1977, Josiah and Constance farmed hay and soybeans and went about their business.

Following passage of the Voting Rights Act in 1965, while Raymond's mother and father were away visiting her aging parents in Cobb County, Georgia, vandals set fire to the little house by Taylor Creek, burning it to the ground and leaving only the stone fireplace standing as a reminder of the 120-plus-year history of the slave cottage.

Chapter 15

Jonny and Raymond were awakened in his hospital room at 6:30 a.m. by the delivery of breakfast. This was followed by the arrival of the hospital physician, Dr. Luisa Valderama. She leafed through Raymond's chart and checked his vital signs.

"Your blood pressure is still a bit high," Dr. Valderama said. After she checked his heart and lungs with a stethoscope, she spoke to Jonny. "Is there any place he needs to be today?"

Jonny regarded her grandfather. "Nope. Not that I know about," she said. "You got any important appointments today, Poppop?" Before he could begin any response, she said, "Nope, all he's got on his calendar is a day without any Oreo cookies." She smiled.

Dr. Valderama did all she could not to laugh out loud. "I believe living in your house might be a most interesting experience, Mr. Steadman," she said. "Your heartbeat is still just a tiny bit off, and your blood pressure is higher than I think it should be. I'd like to keep you one more day, do an EKG and"—she checked Raymond's chart— "monitor blood sugar and triglycerides to determine how to properly medicate your diabetes moving forward. You okay with that?"

"He's fine with that," Jonny said. "Take all the time you need with him."

"Nice to know I got all these bossy women looking after me," he said.

Dr. Valderama replaced his chart on the hook at the foot of the bed. "Yes, it is, Mr. Cheerful. And just so we're clear, another one of 'these bossy women' will be stopping by here within the hour to get that EKG out of the way before lunch." She looked at Jonny. "You don't need to stay here, sweetie," she said. "We bossy women will take very good care of him."

The orderly had brought Jonny a breakfast plate along with Raymond's. When she finished polishing it off, she walked over to Raymond and gave him a kiss on the forehead. "I'm gonna jog home, get cleaned up, and finish my paper, Poppop," she said. "You gonna be alright?"

"I'll be fine, baby," he said. "Guess you have about all you need now, right?"

She nodded. "After last night, I believe I do."

"Well, you get along, then."

The nearly five-mile run left Jonny at peace and ready to move on with things. Since Mr. Hampton had given her the day off from school, she looked forward to getting her paper done before tackling anything else.

She stood in the center of the living room and took in her surroundings. She didn't recall ever having had the house to herself. Her grandfather was always there. She sat down and hammered out the first draft of her assignment. Before going upstairs and taking her shower, she walked onto the back porch and regarded the old tree with newfound interest.

"I guess I understand now why you thought you needed to apologize. What new stuff you got for me today?" she whispered. Jonny collected her backpack. *Heck with it, shower can wait.* She walked out the back door and down the three steps from the porch to the backyard.

Jonny woke with a start and stared at the tree. "What? Seriously? What is it with you?" she shouted.

A voice answered. "What is it with who? Or is it whom?"

She didn't need to turn around to see who'd asked the question. "Hi, Mr. Belvoir," she said. "I was just—"

He waved her off. "How's your grandfather doing? I thought they might have kicked his cranky old behind out of the hospital by now."

"I need to go see him," she said. "He may get to come home either later today or tomorrow."

He gestured for her to join him. "Come on along, then. I'll give you a ride."

After they'd driven for a while, Jonny said, "Mr. Belvoir, I know I've got a couple of years before I have to make a decision, but since you're now Counselor Belvoir and not Senator Belvoir, would you mind counseling me about college?"

Rasmus turned his head slowly, grinning. He nodded a couple of times. "Well, you know, Ms. Carter," he said, "I've certainly got some thoughts, but my normal rate for . . . counseling is about $150 an hour." Jonny's eyes widened. "But for you," he said, "because you are kind of like family, I'll counsel you at the Belvoir family rate."

Jonny started to speak but the retired Senator wasn't done.

"You have to ask yourself a whole lot of questions in order to narrow your . . . let's call it your field of vision. You know what I'm sayin'? For example, what do you want to study? Will you be going on for a graduate degree in something? You want to stay home, or you want to go off and have the whole college experience?"

"Why'd you pick Alcorn?" Jonny asked, stunting Rasmus's inquisition.

He nodded his head a couple of times. "Good question. Simple answer. My choices were limited way back when, due to me having this . . . skin condition."

Jonny looked down at her hands clasped in her lap. "I'm sorry, Mr. Belvoir," she said.

"What you sorry for? I had decent grades. Alcorn said yes to my application, case closed. Only thing that mattered to my parents and me was that Alcorn said yes. You, young lady, have a much wider range of options."

Jonny nodded. They were approaching the hospital parking lot.

"We'll talk more about this," he said to her, "but one thing you need to keep in mind is that your grandfather ain't getting' no younger, and you are his number one priority in the entire universe. He's got to factor into any decision you make."

He started to remove his belt when she asked, "Would you mind reading my history assignment paper, Mr. Belvoir? I want to make sure it's good enough."

"I'd be honored, Jonquil." She handed him her iPad. "Hmmm. Don't anyone use paper anymore, I guess." She showed him how to scroll down using his finger on the screen. "I don't understand all this new stuff." He began reading. Every now and then he turned his head to look at her. When he finished, he let out a deep breath.

"I didn't know about some of this," he said. "Are you sure about what you've written here, Jonquil?"

"Straight from all the horses' mouths, last night," she said. "My grandfather, Mr. Elijah Hampton, and Miss Martha."

He handed Jonny her pad and sat still, staring out at the hospital.

"Well, I guess this makes sense," he said.

"What makes sense?" she asked.

"How nobody knew about much of this," he said. "Only people still alive who knew first-hand are probably those three you just named. I knew about the fire, of course, but nothing about what happened later, with your grandfather. I can't believe he, or Martha, for that matter, never said anything to me. Hell, she worked for me for about a dozen years!"

Jonny explained to him how she'd never even heard of those names before she began work on her history paper. "I guess they really didn't want to talk about it to anyone," she said.

"Everyone's got secrets, Jonquil," he said, absently.

She smiled. "Come on, Mr. Belvoir," she said. "I need to go see my Poppop."

The two old men talked while Jonny sat quietly, editing what she'd written. Her word processing app told her the final version came in at 958 words. "Perfect!" she said, out loud. She was so focused on finishing her paper she didn't register anything the two men had talked about or even that Rasmus had slipped out without saying good-bye.

"What's perfect?" Raymond asked. "'Sides you, of course."

"Yes, I am kind of perfect, aren't I?" she said. "How you doin' old man?"

"You finished with that thing?"

She brought the iPad to him and let him read what she'd written. He nodded a few times. He shook his head once or twice. He handed back her tablet.

"You got it right, Jonny. Hope you're happy."

She smiled. "I am."

They chitchatted for a couple of more minutes until a young, attractive nurse arrived to check Raymond's heart, blood sugar, and blood pressure.

"Well, Mr. Steadman," she announced, while making notations on his chart, "it appears if you can keep these numbers for another twelve hours, you can return home before lunch tomorrow. Now, will you please have the courtesy to introduce me to this lovely young lady?"

"This here is my granddaughter, Jonquil," he said, smiling. "Jonny, this here is the meanest old woman I ever did see in my entire life." They both laughed out loud.

"Asked me for Oreo cookies earlier this afternoon," she said, and introduced herself as Sharon Melville. "Told him he could have all the Oreos he wanted when he was up in heaven with the Lord."

"You are amazing," Jonny said to him. "Thank you, Miss Melville. Old coot doesn't know or care what all is bad for him." The nurse left. Jonny sat on the bed.

"What's on your mind, Jonny?" he asked, reaching for her hand.

"When I walked Martha out last night, she suggested I take another nap down under that old tree," she said.

Her grandfather looked at her. "And . . ."

"I did. This afternoon, before Mr. Belvoir dropped by."

He nodded. "Uh-huh. And . . ."

Jonny hesitated. She knew how he felt about the whole business with the tree. "Why didn't you ever cut that old tree down?"

"I suppose it's 'cause we need reminders, Jonquil. History isn't always pretty, and sometimes, to be perfectly honest, we tend to forget or gloss over some of the more painful stuff, real stuff, about how we got from then to now. In my opinion, and at least on our property, I don't want to forget how things were. It's dangerous to forget. That's why that old tree still stands. Anyway, we both know that it's dying' by its own self. Let's just let it die and then we can decide."

That's why that statue in the park downtown doesn't need to be torn down but maybe moved to a different, more appropriate location, she thought.

Jonny nodded. "Sounds like a plan, old man."

Chapter 16

Wednesday, November 1

Fred talked to himself while walking a trench in the carpet of his parents' living room. He called Todd Hampton a "goddamn traitor to the white race," and told his remaining two friends that he was going to do something about what he referred to as "those fuckin' niggers livin' out on the pike."

"You gotta let this shit go, Fred," Tommy Boggs said. "I want to be friends with you, but you're making it hard. I'm not gonna get in any more trouble 'cause you want to live like it was middle of the last century."

Fred nodded his head. "My grandpa told me when I was nine there'd be people saying stuff like 'all men are created equal.' He said ain't none of it true, that a nigger's life is worth only three-fifths of a white person. It's in the goddamn Constitution, but them bleedin' hearts, they don't tell you that. You need to go and look it up.

"I loved my grandpa. He spent eight years at Parchman Farm for doin' what he thought was right after he saw a colored soldier consorting with a pretty white girl. He had to do something because he said that just wasn't right.

"After he got out and came to live with us, he said, 'Still ain't right, Fred. Hell, that nigger shouldn't even have been allowed to wear the uniform of America's army, but he did. Country's goin' straight to holy hell, Fred.'

"My grandpa said the mixing of races was going to bring on God's apocalypse. When Obama got elected president, grandpa seriously considered committing suicide. He said that nothing like that ever would have happened if the south had won the War of Northern Aggression. He said the best thing ever would've been if the Confederacy had prevailed and the south was in charge. He was right. Niggers would know their damn place now. If it were up to me, I'd kill them all, every last one of them.

"I know you're way too much of a pussy, Boggs, to actually do anything about this stuff," Fred said. "What about you, Glass? You gonna help me get things straight around here?"

Bobby Glass shook his head. "How you gonna get things straight, Fred? What's this girl ever done to you? What's any of these black folks ever done to you? Why are you always so damn angry?"

Fred smiled. "You forget that nigger bitch put me

and Boggs here on the ground? Broke your goddamn nose?" He pointed his finger an inch from the bandage still on Bobby Glass's nose. "We don't do something, those nuts of yours gonna be her next target!" Fred knew he could do what he believed needed to be done alone, but it would be easier if he had at least one more pair of hands. He told them what he had in mind.

Tommy Boggs took his feet off Fred's mother's coffee table and stood up. "I guess you conveniently forget your granddaddy and his friend ended up at Parchman for doing shit like you talking about."

"Don't you be sayin' nothin' bad about my grandfather!" Fred said.

"Look, whatever happened out there that day with that Carter girl, we started it, Fred. You know that. That girl ain't done nothing, not a damn thing, to me I didn't have coming. If you don't shake all this shit loose man, I am done. I am not gonna mess up my whole life so you can get revenge on people ain't never done you no harm." He looked at Bobby Glass. "I'm not telling you what to do, Bobby, but if I was you, I'd let Fred here do whatever he's planning all by his own self. You comin'?"

"I'm sorry, Fred," Bobby said, standing. "We're gonna be seniors next year and I have to get my shit together, so as I can get into Ole Miss. I don't want to get kicked out of school, and I don't want to go to no damn community college, man."

Fred watched his two former friends leave. "Pair of

goddam pussies," he said to the empty room. "Damn right I'll do this myself. Somebody gotta step up, do what's right!"

On Friday afternoon, Tommy Boggs approached Jonny as she left her last class of the day. He walked up to her near the school's bike racks with his hands in the air.

"I'm not here for no trouble, Miz Carter," he said. Jonny fixed her gaze on his hands, which he held out from his body at eye level in a position of surrender.

When it came to trust, Jonny had next to none for Tommy Boggs, Bobby Glass, or especially Fred Holmes. She put her hand up in a 'stop' gesture, telling Tommy to keep his distance. He stayed beyond arm's length and dropped his hands. "That's good," she said, "because I got plenty more of what I gave you before."

"First, I wanna 'pologize for how I been treatin' you," he said. "You don't know me, and I don't know you, and I got no quarrel with you or with black people. I play sports with black guys, and we get on fine. I'm sorry. I deserved what you did to me, and I want to make sure you know that."

Jonny nodded at him. "Yeah, okay. You're sorry. You got anything else?"

"You and your grandfather need to be watchin' yourselves," he said. Jonny stiffened. Tommy put his hands back in the surrender position. "Not anything from me and most probably not anything from Bobby Glass.

But Fred's got some really messed up stuff in his head. And, I don't know why, but he's real, real pissed off, uh, sorry, he's real upset about something you put in that history paper you wrote."

Jesse Hampton was so impressed with her work, he had submitted Jonny's paper to the *Clarion* for consideration in Jeff Dellinger's frequent articles on the history of Pitts County, Mississippi. It also appeared on the school's website.

Jonny nodded. "Whatever I wrote was the truth," she said. "His grandfather and some other jackass started the fire at the *Clarion* newspaper and went to prison for it. That's the truth. That happened."

"Yeah, I don't think that's what it was," Tommy said. "Everybody but me, I guess, knew all about that. This was something you wrote happened that same day out on the pike near where you live."

"Hmmm." *Maybe it wasn't such a good idea for Mr. Dellinger to put the paper up on the Clarion's website.* "Yeah, I know what you're talking about," she said. "Problem is that happened also. Both my grandfather and Mr. Hampton's father confirmed it. So, you can tell your friend, Fred—"

"Oh no," Tommy said, "No! I ain't friends with him no more. He's, I don't know, he's messed up. Just . . . you and your grandfather watch out." He backed away a few steps, nodded his head, gave her a half-hearted wave, and walked away. After a few steps, he stopped and turned back to her.

"Be 'special careful tonight." He shook his head and kept walking.

Jonny shouted at his back. "Okay. Thank you! And I'm sorry for kicking you." She unlocked her bike from the rack. *Not real sorry.*

Jonny rode her bike all the way to the house instead of locking it to one of the fence posts along the pike. Poppop was on the porch.

"How you doin' baby girl," he said to her. She let her bike fall to the ground.

"Poppop, we gotta talk," she said and launched into a breathless recap of what Tommy Boggs had said to her.

"That's what he said? Be careful tonight?"

"Yep. What are we gonna do, Poppop?"

He called Elijah Hampton.

"Turtle? You okay?" Elijah asked.

"So far," he said. He repeated to Elijah what Jonny had told him. Jonny stood next to him, nodding her head, then paced around the living room.

Raymond put his hand over the mouthpiece of the phone. "Girl, you gonna walk holes in the rug you don't sit down. Okay … okay," Raymond said into the phone. "Yeah, okay. See you in a bit."

Raymond called 9-1-1 and told the operator he had reason to believe someone might be coming to his house to cause harm to him and his granddaughter. "No, not now, not yet," he said. "Okay, thank you." He looked at Jonny. "It's not an emergency yet, so she's connecting me with the sheriff's office."

Raymond explained the situation to the deputy who answered the call at the Pitts County sheriff's office. Then, he explained it again to someone else. By the time the call ended, he'd told the story to three different people.

"What's happening?" Jonny asked him.

"Damn if I know, Jonny. They gonna add extra patrols up and down the pike and, if they can, they'll put a car up near the end of the driveway. Tell you the truth, I ain't counting on any of their help."

They sat quietly in the living room, mostly just looking at each other. They both jumped up when they heard a vehicle approach. Elijah Hampton, his son, Jesse, and Jesse's son, Todd jumped out of Elijah's truck. All three were carrying rifles. Elijah had two, one of which was a big 12-gauge. They walked up the steps to the porch.

"Damn," Raymond said. "Y'all obviously expecting big trouble here."

Elijah said, "I brought this one for you, Turtle. You teach your granddaughter how to shoot yet?" They both shook their heads.

"I kind of hope she never needs to know how to use any kind of gun," he said.

She threw him a skeptical look. "Can't be that hard. Y'all seem to know how to use 'em," she said.

"Maybe after all this stuff is done, I'll teach you how to hit a target," Todd Hampton said. "You're right. It ain't hard."

She smiled at him. "That'd be fine, Todd."

They took seats around the living room. Jesse Hampton coughed the room to attention. "I just told my father about this," he said. "At first I dismissed it as teenage nonsense, but after Dad told me what you said Tommy Boggs told Jonquil, I thought it best we take this seriously."

"Take what seriously?" Jonny asked.

"I probably shouldn't have gotten so enthusiastic with your history paper," he said to her. "But it was so good and, really, so important I just thought—"

Raymond waved him off. "What you need to tell us, Jesse?"

"I guess we all know Fred Holmes is a little . . . off about race relations," he said. "But he's also not all that bright of a light. And that's . . . that's potentially a dangerous combination. After an eleventh-grade history class, Fred stayed behind and lit into me about Jonny's paper. He told me it was a bunch of lies, and that if people keep telling lies about his grandfather, something bad is going to happen. I pressed him to tell me what, exactly, the lies were, but he wasn't really coherent. He screamed at me for believing black people instead of what he called 'my own people.'"

Raymond told the group about his frustrating and unproductive call to the sheriff's office.

Elijah stood. "We'll see about that. Can I use your telephone, Turtle?"

Raymond waved at him. Elijah punched in a number. "Sheriff there? Tell him it's Elijah." He listened for a moment. Then he nodded his head. "Yes, Elijah Hampton. And I wouldn't waste his time or my own time if it wasn't important."

Jonny went into the kitchen and collected red Solo cups. She brought them into the living room, along with a pitcher of sweet tea.

"I'm fine, Albert," Elijah said into the phone. "Listen here. I think you need to get your ass out of your office and get into your cruiser and get over here to Raymond Steadman's house out on the pike. You know where it is?" He went on to explain the potential threat from Fred Holmes.

"Yes, I know." A short pause. "Yeah, that's right, Albert. Maybe bring a deputy or two along with you." Another short pause. "Yeah, and one more thing. Maybe you can bring a couple of pizza pies from that Italian place near Lois's Coffee Shop? We gonna be here all night if we have to, and we're gonna need some food. I'll pay you back for it." He hung up, looked at Raymond and shook his head.

"I'm sorry, Turtle," Elijah said. "In this messed up world and, especially, in politics and, double especially, here in the south, it's not what you ask for, and it's not who you ask. It's who asks. And, in case you haven't made the connection just yet, our fine sheriff's daddy was that other piece of garbage out here all them years ago. I should've just put bullets into all those yahoos back then, including my own idiot brother. None of this nonsense would be infesting our little community. Hell, they all dead now anyway."

Raymond cocked his head and stared at Elijah. "You tellin' me—"

Elijah gestured for him to calm down. "Look, Turtle, I am not my brother or my daddy, right? And Albert Collins is not his daddy. Hell, Dickie Holmes got racists come before him and after him, but he and Winnie are fine, normal people. You take my word, Albert Collins is gonna do what's right. And before all's said and done here tonight, we'll make sure young Fred learns a lesson he should have learned a long damn time ago."

Chapter 17

Jesse Hampton walked toward the front door. He signaled Jonny to join him. She followed him to the end of the porch. She remained quiet while he took in his surroundings. "You know, I've never been to your house before," he said.

"Really? Your uncle owned it, back when all that stuff happened."

He smiled. "I know, but I wasn't even born until several years after your grandfather's people moved into it, back in the 1960s."

"Hmmm," she said. "I guess you're right."

"I never knew my uncle Sam," he said. "Maybe I'm better off for that."

She smiled at him. "Thanks for coming out to-night." They continued an easy silence for a few more moments.

"Do you and your grandfather ever sit out here at night?" he asked her.

"You mean, like, late at night? In the dark?"

He nodded. "Yes, that's exactly right. How dark does it get?"

"Well, unless we put our porch light on it gets really dark," she said. "There's a light up where the driveway meets the pike, but it's nearly a quarter mile, well . . . about four hundred meters, actually, up that way, and there's all the trees."

"That's what I thought," he said. "I have an idea." They went back inside.

"What was that all about," Elijah asked his son.

"Wanted to see how dark it gets out there," he said. They all turned toward the door at the sound of cars coming up the drive. Albert Collins eased his ample body out of the lead car. Two other department vehicles followed behind him. The sheriff of Pitts County and four of his deputies walked onto the porch. Elijah opened the door.

"Thanks for coming out, Albert," he said. "And thanks for bringing your deputies."

The sheriff nodded. "Elijah."

One of the deputies carried four pizza boxes. Elijah looked at Raymond. He nodded and Elijah gestured for them to come inside. Albert Collins walked directly up to Raymond and extended his hand. Raymond stood and took the hand of the son of one of the men who'd tried to lynch him all those years ago.

"Mr. Steadman," the sheriff said, "first of all, I need to apologize to you. I was in my office when you called, but I have some folks working for me who think it's their job in life to prevent my constituents from talking directly to me. I hope you'll accept my apology."

Raymond smiled. "Not necessary, sheriff," he said. "I'm glad you're here and that y'all brought along that pizza with you. Jonny, we got plates and napkins and more tea for these gentlemen?" She went into the kitchen and retrieved two jugs of sweet tea and more cups.

"Anyone need ice?" she asked.

One of the deputies removed a ball cap. "Oops, sorry, ma'am," Raymond said. "Gentlemen *and* lady."

She smiled and nodded. "Deputy Miller, sir," she said. The others introduced themselves. They all started in on the pies, except the sheriff.

"As you can see, Mr. Steadman, it's a different department today than it was back when . . . well, I don't need to tell you," he said. Two of the deputies he'd brought with him were young, strong black men, not unlike Raymond was in May of 1960. "So, what's going on here, Elijah?"

Elijah looked around the room. "You know, I think maybe Jonquil ought to lay out the situation. Jonny, can you do that, please?"

Jonny nodded. She wasn't sure but she thought that might have been the first time Elijah Hampton called her "Jonny." She recounted her meeting earlier in the afternoon with Tommy Boggs. She included references to her earlier run-ins with Holmes, Boggs, and Glass. Todd Hampton confirmed her story. She looked at her teacher. "You want to tell them what happened after class today?" she asked. Jesse repeated details of his encounter with Fred Holmes.

The sheriff listened attentively. "You know," he said, after they'd stopped speaking, "grandparents can have a good influence on their grandkids, like Mr. Steadman here and like you, Elijah." He settled his gaze on Jonny and Todd seated together on the window seat. "You two are credits to this community. Unfortunately, young Mr. Holmes got the worst possible influences from his grandfather. He and my own father used to be friends, but I just hope you know he doesn't represent anything close to most . . . well, of many people at all here in Pitts County today.

"In my job, we typically encounter people at their worst. I'm sorry you had to go through that, Miss Carter, although I'm glad to learn you got your licks in on those boys. None of them should have done any of that, but Fred Holmes appears to be the problem we have to deal with today." He looked at Raymond. "I'm happy to go pick that boy up and read him the riot act, Mr. Steadman, but from a law enforcement point of view, he really hasn't done anything bad enough yet to be arrested." Raymond and Elijah both started to speak but were interrupted.

"Excuse me, Pop—Mr. Steadman," Jesse said. "Can I run something by the sheriff first?"

Raymond gestured for Jonny's teacher to continue. Elijah nodded. "Go ahead, son."

Jesse laid out the simple plan he'd dreamed up when he and Jonny went out on the porch. When Jesse finished, Jonny watched as he, Todd, Sheriff Collins, her grandfather, and the four deputies moved to the front porch. She heard them talking about Jesse's idea if and when Fred Holmes showed up.

Elijah was inside with her, working on a third slice of pepperoni and spinach pizza. He smiled at her. "I suppose you got a little more than you bargained for with this history paper my son gave you to do," he said.

She grabbed the last slice of supreme and sat next to him. "Few days ago, my grandfather said something to me like, 'You don't know what you know, and you don't know what you don't know.' It's only been a little over two weeks since we got that assignment. I have learned so much since then."

He smiled at her. "Until this evening I doubt any of these people," he waved his hand toward the door, "have ever been on this property, never mind inside this house."

"You must have been here before," she said, "since your brother lived in this house."

"My brother," he said, shaking his head. "Do you know your scripture, Jonquil?"

She looked down. "Not as well as I probably should."

"'There are none so blind as those who will not see,'" he said. "Traces back to the book of Jeremiah. My late brother would not see." She nodded. "It was in this house, back there"—he waved his hand in the direction of the kitchen— "he finally came to terms with who he was and what he did."

Jonny stood up and moved in front of Elijah.

"I now know what he did, but what's more important is, I now know what you did," she said. He began to wave her off, but she shook her head. "Don't you dare, sir! You saved my grandfather's life that night. If you didn't do what you did, he'd have died. That means my mother would never have been born, which means I would not have been born." He stood. Tears streamed from his tired eyes down his wrinkled cheeks.

"Never thought of it that way," he said, his voice breaking. "Your grandfather didn't deserve none of that. He was a good man then, and he's a good man now."

"Thank you," Jonny said, "for what you did and what you just said." She put her arms around him while they both wept.

They'd disengaged by the time the others stepped back inside. Darkness was settling in. They waited patiently until Deputy Miller, who'd been standing guard on the porch, reported seeing car headlights up the driveway by the Pitts Taylor Pike.

Fred Holmes knew he was drunk. He originally wanted to use the bottle of Jack Daniels he'd managed to purchase from a package store just over the state line in Tennessee for a practice run. He'd planned to launch it through the big plate glass window on the South Street side of the *Clarion* building, just as his grandfather and Arthur Collins had done all those years ago. That would teach them a lesson for printing lies about his grandfather.

Instead, he managed to drink or spill more than two thirds of the bottle. At first, he convinced himself what was left, properly fused and lit, would do the trick. Upon impaired reflection, he decided to follow the recipe employed by his grandfather. He'd gone to the shed where his father kept his lawn equipment and filled the near-empty bottle of Jack with gasoline.

"Don't never ask yourself why, Fred," his grandpa had told him before he died. "And don't let no one else ask you why, either. 'Why' is the enemy of what you know in your heart is right. This is how it's supposed to be, Fred. America's supposed to be white. ALL white. Period." His grandfather had loaded the *White American Report* podcast on Fred's phone and showed it to him. "This here thing will keep you on track, moving in the right direction, doing God's work so's to get us to an ALL white America." *WAR* constituted the most hardcore of white-nationalist information to be found on the internet. It was another of his grandfather's gifts.

As darkness descended on the pike, Fred sat in the cab of his truck listening through ear buds to the latest installment of the WAR. When it ended, he exited his truck and wobbled around to the passenger door.

He checked his pocket for his grandfather's Zippo lighter and flicked it to make sure it was working. He removed the screw top on the Jack Daniels bottle and inserted the fuel-soaked rag into the tea-colored mixture of whiskey and gasoline and stumbled in the general direction of the Steadman house.

It took Fred nearly three minutes to navigate the driveway. He stood, in total darkness, ten yards from the front door. He could see light through the front window but nothing else.

"I'm doin' this for you, grandpa," he mumbled. "And for America. And for . . ." He removed the lighter from his pocket and ignited the rag.

As soon as the rag caught fire, four deputies moved in from all sides, guns drawn, screaming as loud as they could for Fred to drop to his knees. Instead, disoriented by the noise coming at him from all directions, Fred dropped the bottle at his feet and managed immediately to set his shoes and the cuffs of his tan chinos on fire. Sheriff Collins came down the steps with a large, red fire extinguisher and saved a screaming and thrashing Fred Holmes from setting himself completely on fire.

"You are under arrest, you stupid son of a bitch," the sheriff said, shaking his head.

After the chaos of the moment passed, Sheriff Collins handcuffed Fred Holmes, read him his rights, told him everything he was charged with, from public and underage intoxication, all the way up to and including possession of an illegal weapon, attempted arson, attempted murder and, potentially, a hate crime. He sat him down in the back seat of one of the cruisers, watched over by two armed deputies, both black.

"Every now and then, a good plan turns out to actually be a good plan," the sheriff said in thanks to Jesse Hampton. "I guess we could have stopped it before it started, but who knows? In a week, a month, a year, he probably would have tried something equally stupid again, and we can't be here all the time based on 'probably.' This way, we've got young Fred on a variety of charges with several credible eyewitnesses and a couple of cell phone videos. I feel bad for his parents, but I've got a sense they know their son is a couple sandwiches shy of a picnic. What I know is, this stuff needs to stop, as much as we can help make it stop." The sheriff turned to Raymond, Jonny, Elijah, Jesse, and Todd.

"I look forward to seeing you all again but under different circumstances." He turned to his deputies. "Come on, y'all. We're done here."

Chapter 18

Thursday, November 30

Jonny and Raymond walked up South Street toward the park, where they'd made plans to connect with Martha, Rasmus, Elijah, and Todd Hampton. Any remaining humidity from the unseasonably mild fall had gone north and turned into rain over western Tennessee.

Jonny was thinking about her recent weekend visit to Ole Miss. She'd been invited by Alison Wynn, a grad student, who'd come to Vosalia to interview and record Jonny, Raymond, and Elijah for a documentary film she was making about the civil rights movement in Mississippi between 1954 and 1965. In Oxford, Jonny met the others in Ms. Wynn's group, and got to tour the campus and meet informally with the head coach of the Ole Miss women's track and field team. She lit up when she learned that the coach of the whole team, not just the women, was an African American woman, and that she knew Jonny's name and how well she'd done at regionals. The coach knew Jonny had collected a first-place medal in the 400-meter hurdles, achieving a personal best time of 57.62 seconds. She also knew Jonny had earned a first-place medal anchoring the 4 x 400-meter relay team. She still had some distance to go to catch Sanya Richards's high school record, but she was gaining ground.

"When it's time for you to consider college, Ms. Carter," the coach had said, while still holding Jonny's hand, "please look here first, and then look here last."

Answers to Jonny's questions about college were suddenly coming into sharper focus. Maybe she'd look into journalism as a major now that Jeff Dellinger had offered her a summer internship at the newspaper.

"I don't think you ever did tell me what you learned last time you took a nap under that old tree, Jonny," Raymond said, breaking into her thoughts. "You gettin' shy now you're a full-grown almost fifteen-year-old?"

She laughed at him. "I've never been shy, Poppop," she said. "I am almost fifteen now, but I don't think I'm full grown just yet, am I?"

He nodded at her. "You're full grown enough to dance around answering my question, young lady. And, you grown enough to be spending a whole lot of your time with young Mr. Hampton." She shot him a sidelong glance.

"Okay, okay, I'm just sayin' . . ." He chuckled.

"You know, Poppop, that last time I had a hard time falling asleep under the tree."

He stopped and looked at her. "When did you ever have a hard time falling asleep, Jonquil? You're the one always said you could sleep standing up."

"Well, I did eventually fall asleep, but I don't know what to make of it," she said. "All I got that day was the tree telling me 'thank you' and then, 'Now, everything is as it should be.'"

"Tree said 'thank you' and 'Now everything is as it should be'?"

She nodded her head. "That's it. Word for word."

He smiled and laughed. "Damn tree's gettin' all polite and philosophical in its old age."

"I guess," she said. She put her arm through his and they walked together up South Street to Harold Christianson Park.

Jonny and Raymond arrived at the park just before Elijah Hampton and his grandson showed up. Martha and Rasmus were already there. Elijah quickly engaged with Mr. Belvoir.

"You know, Erasmus," he began, "I'm not sure all of this was entirely necessary. While that statue's presence certainly may have aroused sensitivities, especially after all that ignorance and unpleasantness up in Charlottesville, are we as a society now expected to remove anything from public view that upsets any of us?" The two gentlemen moved away from the others, engaged in a conversation involving the relative importance of retaining uncomfortable vestiges of the past in the face of rampant political correctness. Raymond watched his two old friends go at it.

"Any time those two end up in the same zip code, civil war breaks out again. Keep your distance, Jonquil."

"Oh, fiddle faddle, Turtle, uh, Raymond," Martha said. "Intelligent discussion of important matters keeps the mind nimble and stimulates the soul." She smiled at Jonny. "Why Jonquil Carter, you look especially lovely today. I'm told your paper for Mr. Hampton's history class turned out well. Is that correct?"

Jonny beamed. "Got an A, Miss—Martha," she said. She recounted how her teacher had posted the paper on the school's website and had sent it to Jeff Dellinger, who included it in his monthly look back at Pitts County history. "Mr. Hampton told me he passed it on to the university for a competition they're sponsoring. He said if it wins, I could get some scholarship money." She told Martha about the documentary film Alison Wynn was producing, and that she'd probably love to talk to Martha and Mr. Belvoir.

Following two additional, contentious town council meetings, at which what seemed like the entire population of Vosalia each had a moment to weigh in on the subject, there were surprisingly few people on hand for the actual physical removal of Johnny Reb.

The council had voted three to one, with Councilman Townsend abstaining, to relocate Johnny Reb to the Confederate cemetery north of the town limits but still in Pitts County, adjacent to the Pitts Taylor Community College campus.

In a separate vote, the Council unanimously decided to table the 55-22 Company's request to develop what had, over time, evolved into a project containing a greater number of residential units rising over an even larger number of street-level commercial spaces.

"Stores, offices, and apartments won't happen during my term," Mayor Edwards wistfully told Jeff Dellinger in an interview for the *Clarion*. "Too much density for our little town." The 55-22 people had offered to call the project Edwards Town Place, but even that ego bribe didn't carry the day.

This meant that, for the foreseeable future, a lovely green space in the center of the downtown Vosalia core would exist without a statue that upset and offended a sizeable number of local residents.

Erasmus Belvoir now watched from a bench alongside Martha Plemmons sharing a bag of boiled peanuts. Jonny sat with them. A handful of grumpy women from the Daughters of the Confederacy, along with several people from the town's Historical Preservation Board, also were on hand. "Johnny Reb will still have a powerful presence in Pitts County," Georgia Lee Townsend gushed. "Our nameless soldier will stand in oversight of those who fought and died for the Confederate cause. He survives, Delia, and that's what's important."

Delia Scott, from the Daughters of the Confederacy, shook her head and stared at her former ally. "This is soul crushing, Georgia Lee," Delia said. "Might as well just erase the whole episode and consign all those dead and our unnamed soldier to the dustbin of yesterday's trash. It's embarrassing, and it's all his fault." Delia pointed and tossed her head in the general direction of Erasmus. "I'm shocked he doesn't use this cultural blasphemy as a platform to run for mayor!"

Martha Plemmons smiled at her former boss. "Are you contemplating a return to the arena of politics, Rasmus?" she asked.

Belvoir threw a side-eye at Delia Scott. "I hadn't. Not until now," he said. "Might do it just to grind her lily-white gullet."

"Well," Martha said, "Allow me to be the first to donate to your campaign." She handed him a bottle of spring water.

"I guess it's official, then," he said, shaking his head.

The workers from the town, under HPB supervision, did a great job keeping Johnny Reb intact, but didn't do quite as well with the base of the statue. The life-sized soldier, his rifle held at the ready, had been carefully removed from the six-foot concrete cube on which he'd stood for more than a century. The town council, in a move designed to placate those most vehemently opposed to doing anything with Mr. Reb other than leaving him in peace, agreed to fund a new bronze plaque to be affixed to the base. However, since the existing base demonstrated a clear lack of structural integrity following removal of the soldier, a new base would surely come up for discussion at next month's meeting.

Elijah, Todd, and Raymond joined the others, taking seats on an adjacent bench. "Has there been anything new with regard to that sad, pathetic Holmes boy?" Martha asked no one in particular.

"Actually, I got a call yesterday from the sheriff," Raymond said. "You were right, Elijah, about Albert Collins. He wasted no time conferring with Fred's parents and with the Pitts County district attorney. Since Fred was six months shy of his eighteenth birthday when he did what he did, it was determined he'd be treated as a juvenile if he and his parents agreed to a sentence of four years in the medium-security detention facility in Hernando."

"Did you remind our sheriff exactly what that young moron tried to do?" Elijah asked. "I'd have charged him as an adult, tried his ass, and made sure he ended up in the same damn cell as his dumbass grandfather did down at Parchman."

Martha looked at Elijah with some skepticism. "Oh, you're not nearly as hard a man as you'd like to portray, Mr. Hampton," she said. "The boy had his mind poisoned by that horrible grandfather of his."

"I love you, Miss Plemmons," Elijah said, "but that

liberal heart of yours gonna be a big disappointment to you someday. You know what they say, right?"

"No sir, I do not "know what they say." Pray tell, what do "they" say?"

Elijah Hampton looked a broad grin at Martha Plemmons. "They say a conservative is a liberal who has been mugged!"

Even Jonny had a good laugh.

Workers collected all the detritus from the base of the statue of Johnny Reb and hauled it to the bed of a county truck. Where it might end up was anyone's guess.

"He asked me if I was alright with what they had planned for young Fred," Raymond said.

"And he asked me," said Jonny. She'd moved from where she was sitting to a seat next to Todd.

"Well, you and Todd had already inflicted some punishment on the boy," Elijah said. "What'd you tell the sheriff, Raymond?"

"I told him I didn't think four years was long enough," he said. "The district attorney told me in order to try for a longer sentence he'd have to charge him as an adult, and in that case, there'd likely be a trial."

"And, at a trial, anything could happen," Rasmus chimed in. Raymond pointed a finger at him and nodded his head. "They could contend he was drunk, which he was, and didn't know what he was doing, which he probably didn't, and he could quite possibly have simply walked away with a stern reprimand from the judge."

The six of them looked on as others began clearing out of the park. The only reminder of Johnny Reb's presence was an area of dead grass in the middle of an otherwise clear green space.

"You know" Raymond said, "us getting all that stuff out and off our chests has hopefully left me with maybe a tad of forgiveness. No sense in ruining another life over all this nonsense if we don't have to."

Jonny nodded her head and smiled. "Besides," she said, "he'll still have me to contend with when he gets out."

That got smiles and laughs from the adults. Todd put his arm on the back of the bench, around Jonny. The others noted this, and exchanged knowing looks, head nods, and 'uh-huhs.'

"Y'all remember," Rasmus said, "this here is still Vosalia, Mississippi." Raymond and Martha looked at each other and smiled.

"That's very astute of you, Senator Belvoir," Martha said. "It's also approaching the latter part of the second decade of the twenty-first century." She leaned over and pecked Raymond on his cheek.

The six of them, young and old, black and white, enjoyed a raucous laugh, as they sat, alone, together, in Harold Christiansen Park in downtown Vosalia, Mississippi.

EPILOGUE

The Following Spring

Jonny woke on a Sunday morning in late April to the aroma of sweet sausage sizzling in a well-seasoned cast iron skillet on top of the stove. After a pit stop, she threw on sweats and bounded down the stairs. Raymond was putting the sausage onto plates piled high with scrambled eggs, cantaloupe, fried potatoes with onions, and sliced tomatoes.

"Yum!" she said. "Now that's what I call breakfast!" She went to the refrigerator, grabbed a carton of milk, and poured herself a tall glass. "What's the occasion, Poppop?"

"No occasion," he said. "Just Sunday. Figure we'll go to church, and then walk around town a bit. Maybe go visit Martha. How's that work for you?"

Jonny beamed at him. "I do believe you are sweet on Miss Martha," she said.

He shook his head. "Couple of people can't go and visit someone without you making a whole big thing out of it? Besides, how many times did young Todd Hampton drop you off after school this week? Four times? Five? So, don't you go worrying none about me and Miss Martha Plemmons, young lady. Okay? You got your own stuff goin' on, and don't tell me you don't." It was time for Raymond to change the subject. "He finished teaching you how to shoot?"

"Not yet. I'm doing pretty good with a long gun," she said. "Now he's showing me how to use a handgun."

He looked at her for a long moment. "I guess it's okay. You shootin' out back on his property or you going to a range?"

"Doing both," she said. "In exchange, I'm teaching him how to dance." They smiled at one another. "I think he's going to ask me to his prom, Poppop." she said.

Raymond looked at her and sighed. "Just you be careful, Jonquil," he said. "And you tell him he needs to be careful, too. This is still Vosalia, Mississippi, and some folks still got a ways to go. You hear what I'm saying?"

"You know, Poppop, there's something I still don't understand about all that happened on May 26," Jonny said.

"Just one thing?" he asked, smiling.

She put down her fork and threw him a face. "Probably not, old man," she said. "But for now . . ."

"What do you want to know, Miss Carter?"

She looked around the dining room for a moment, clearly unsure of how to ask him about what was on her mind. Finally, she stopped and stared at him.

"The one guy, Holmes, right?"

He nodded. "Richard Holmes," he said. "Your boy Fred's grandfather." He shook his head. "Birds of a damn feather."

"How is it," she asked, "you never, I don't know . . ." Raymond nodded and signaled for her to continue. "I mean, you never ran into him around Vosalia? You know, after he got out of prison, and you got out of the army. How can that be? It's a small town, a small county." She cocked her head.

Raymond looked out the window to his left and then looked at the door to the bathroom, off to his right.

"I don't know what to tell you, Jonny," he said. "Yeah, I saw him here and there. What was I going to do? Run up, throw my arms around him, say something like, 'Hey, Richard, long time no see. You doin' okay, buddy?'"

"He tried to lynch you, Poppop!"

"I know, Jonquil, I was there, remember? We had nothing to say to each other. I doubt after all that time he even recognized me. You know, to some white people, we all look alike, right?"

"I don't know, Poppop. I might have wanted to . . . something."

Raymond shook his head and smiled. "You've known me all your life, right? Am I the kind of person to just walk up to someone and start poundin' on him? Even someone who, you know, did what he did. Uh, uh. 'Sides . . ."

"'Sides, what?" she asked him. "What?"

Raymond pulled himself up, refilled his coffee cup and took a sip. He sighed. "Look here" he said, "there was this one time, I don't remember exactly when. I'd walked up the drive to the mailbox, look out onto the road, and he goes by in a truck. He's heading into town, I guess. Must have been living with his son's family a few miles up the pike near the county line. Drivin' a red F-150 if I recall. Gotta be . . . I don't know how long ago . . . before you were even born. He slows down and we just look at each other."

"That's what you did?" Jonny asked, incredulous. "You looked at each other?"

Raymond laughed. "What have you got going on in that head o' yours, Jonny? Yeah, we looked at each other. He drove by and I took the mail out the mailbox and walked back home. End of story. We saw each other once in 1960 and then once years, maybe decades later, for a moment. He died, probably about seven, eight years ago. We never saw each other after that, and I promise you, we ain't gonna see each other ever again."

"So, you're telling me there was never any, I don't know, confrontation? Resolution? Words? Revenge? Nothing?"

Raymond shrugged his shoulders and shook his head. "No, darlin', nothin'. That's all I got for you, Jonny. Trust me, you know everything about May 26, 1960, and then some. Like I said, end of story."

They sat quietly at the kitchen table for a moment, locked hands, and closed their eyes. Jonny offered grace.

Raymond started eating his breakfast when he noticed his granddaughter looking at him with a smile on her face. "Something amusing you, young lady?"

She nodded. "Uh-huh. I remembered something from when you were in the hospital and you, and Martha and Mr. Hampton told me about what happened on May 26, 1960."

He looked at her. "Okay."

"You said, you were going to tell me something for the second time. You remember that?"

It was his turn to smile. "Yes, Jonquil, I do."

"I think I would have remembered you telling me all that about the *Clarion* fire, the attempted lynching, the whole business with Elijah, and with Sam Hampton."

He stopped eating his breakfast and turned to her. "Do you remember me telling you that when you was a baby, I used to walk around this house carrying you, talking to you, telling you all kinds of stories and all kinds of nonsense so you'd drink your bottle or fade off to sleep?"

Jonny laughed out loud. "Are you telling me you told me that whole story when I was a little baby?"

"That's exactly what I'm telling you."

They spent a few more moments taking in breakfast. Then Jonny put her fork down, leaned in, and gave her grandfather a stern look. She wasn't quite ready to buy.

"I don't know, Poppop," she said.

"Okay, let's try this," he said, holding one of his hands out, palm up. "This comes out of the file marked 'common sense.' Say I told you all about this when you were a baby, it got filed away somewhere in that smart, beautiful brain of yours, and you somehow recalled some pieces of it when you fell asleep thinking about that assignment." He put his other hand out, palm up, "Or, say you fell asleep by the tree, and the tree talked to you in one of your dreams and told you it was sorry for something it did, something that happened or didn't happen back on May 26, 1960." He moved his hands up and down, as if measuring the relative weight of the two possibilities.

"Poppop," she said, "I don't have any memory of anything like that before you and Martha and Mr. Hampton told me all that stuff in the hospital."

He nodded again. "Okay, okay, wait a minute," he said. "You like baseball, right?"

"I like all sports," she said. "You know that."

"I do. What team do you root for?"

"The Braves. You know that, too."

"I do. Why you root for the Braves?"

"Because they're like . . . our local team," she said.

"Why's that? We're closer to St. Louis than we are to Atlanta," he said. "Why don't you root for the Cardinals?"

Jonny pulled her iPad out of her backpack and spent a few moments with Google. "Hmmm. I did not know that." She looked at Raymond. He was smiling, and clearly enjoying himself. "Come on, Poppop."

"Okay, okay. Let me ask you this. If you were ever going to join into the military service" he said, "what branch would you go into? Army? Navy?"

"Hmmm," she said again. "Haven't really ever thought about doing that."

"Hypothetical speaking, of course, because you're going to college and you're gonna be an Olympic athlete. But hypothetical speaking."

She thought for a moment. "I guess . . . I don't know . . . I'd probably pick the Marines."

He nodded. "Of course, you would. But why?"

"I don't know," she said. "Maybe because my father was a marine?"

He smiled and put his hands out, palms up. "There you have it, young lady."

"There I have what? What the Sam Hill are you talking about, old man?"

"I told you when you was small, small as that bread box over there, all about the Atlanta Braves," he said. "And I told you, when you was only a little bigger than that bread box, about how your daddy picked the Marines because he wanted to take advantage of their training. I told you all that while you were under a year old, holding you in my arms, walking around this room."

She put down her fork, nodded, stroked her chin, pursed her lips, nodded again, shook her head, and then smiled at him.

"What are you doing, Jonquil Carter?"

"I . . . am cogitating!" He laughed out loud.

She started to speak again when something outside the kitchen window caught her eye. She put down her fork and walked over to the window. After nearly a minute, just standing and staring out the window, Raymond called to her.

"What you studyin' on back there that's more important than finishing this wonderful breakfast I prepared for us?"

"Poppop, come on over here," she said, softly. "You need to see this." He sighed, pushed his chair away from the table, and walked to his granddaughter. She was still staring out the window.

"You see what I see?" she asked.

"Yeah, I see that big, old, near-dead—well, will you look at that?"

"I am looking at that," she said. "Are you looking at that?"

It was a beautiful spring morning. The sun was shining, and the sky was blue and clear of clouds. A gentle breeze caught some of the high branches of the big, old oak they both were certain was dying just a few short months ago.

Jonny said, "'Now everything is as it should be.' That's what I dreamed the tree said to me." She smiled. "Last time we talked, that is."

"Uh-huh" Raymond said. He put his hand on her shoulder.

The tree was resplendent; it was filled with tiny new leaves. Except for their fluttering in the breeze, the way the sun hit the tree gave it the appearance of a landscape painting in different shades of brown and green. Where the previous fall the branches were nearly empty, there was an emerging lushness to the huge old tree.

"I haven't seen it look like that in years," Raymond said. Jonny had never seen it like how it appeared on this lovely spring day.

She looked at him. "Poppop," she said, "maybe everything that happened last fall needed to happen, so this could happen. Maybe that tree wasn't ready to die or be cut down."

"Sure does look that way, Jonny," he said.

"What do you think about all this?" she asked him.

"I got no earthly idea what I think, Jonny," he said. "But I do believe maybe it's time for me to build you that swing you been wanting."

Jonny smiled at him. "That would be nice, Poppop. "Real nice."

"You know," he said, "we can discuss whether the tree told you all that stuff or if it was all already up in there in that pretty little head of yours and only needed a little help getting out. I don't really guess we'll ever know for sure or that it really matters."

"Miss Martha told me one time," she said, "there are questions to which there are no answers, and there are problems to which there are no solutions." Raymond nodded and smiled.

The old, near-dead oak tree was very much alive.

End

Acknowledgements

The author would like to thank so, so many people who have knowingly or otherwise supported this effort, including the Katz, Medlar, Foster, Diehn, and Van Oss families; friends and colleagues in both western North Carolina and central Florida; professors and fellow students at Valencia College, Rollins College, and Western Carolina University; and even a few from long ago in Brooklyn, New York, and the United States Air Force. Some may recognize pieces and aspects of themselves on these and future pages, while others may wonder why they've been forgotten. They haven't.

Thanks to Robert Kenney of Thoughtful Editing, Victoria Griffin, and Anna Krusinski from Blue Pen. Thanks to Ron Rash, Pam Duncan, Bob Morris, and Steven Cooper for their wisdom, advice, counsel, and encouragement through the years. Special thanks always to Lynn for putting up with all the hours of closed doors and both quiet keystrokes and noisy grumbling emanating from the back room.

About the Author

Bruce F. Katz – Bud to his friends – is author of the business biography, *When Your Name Is On the Door*, along with five novels, a novella, and more than a dozen short stories. He was graduated Magna Cum Laude from Western Carolina University with a BA in English. He's a former strategic communication, mass media, advertising and public relations executive living with his wife, Lynn, a retired defense and aerospace industry executive, in Highlands, North Carolina.

www.ingramcontent.com/pod-product-compliance
Lightning Source LLC
Chambersburg PA
CBHW060533160726
47991CB00001B/305